THE HOUSE AT HUNGRY MOUNTAIN

THE HOUSE AT HUNGRY MOUNTAIN

Des Morley

Chivers Press   •   G.K. Hall & Co.
Bath, England   Waterville, Maine USA

This Large Print edition is published by Chivers Press, England, and by G.K. Hall & Co., USA.

Published in 2002 in the U.K. by arrangement with Robert Hale Ltd.

Published in 2002 in the U.S. by arrangement with Dorian Literary Agency.

U.K. Hardcover   ISBN 0–7540–4748–2 (Chivers Large Print)
U.K. Softcover   ISBN 0–7540–4749–0 (Camden Large Print)
U.S. Softcover   ISBN 0–7838–9666–2 (Nightingale Series Edition)

The text of this Large Print edition is unabridged.
Other aspects of the book may vary from the original edition.

Set in 16 pt. New Times Roman.

Printed in Great Britain on acid-free paper.

British Library Cataloguing in Publication Data available

Library of Congress Cataloging-in-Publication Data

Morley, Des.
    The house at Hungry Mountain / Des Morley.
        p. cm.
    ISBN 0–7838–9666–2 (lg. print : sc : alk. paper)
    1. Easter Island—Fiction. 2. Large type books. I. Title.
PR6063.O7443 H68 2001
823'.914—dc21

2001039976

This is for my sister
Daphne Truth Piercy

PASCUA

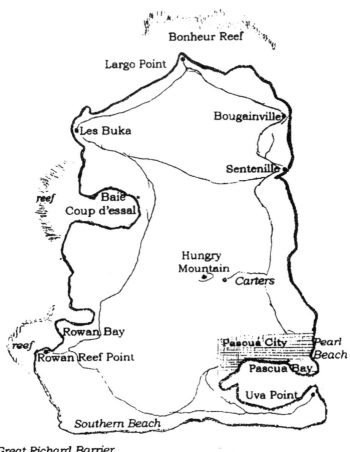

Bonheur Reef

Largo Point

Bougainville

Les Buka

Sentenille

reef

Baie
Coup d'essal

Hungry
Mountain

Carters

Rowan Bay

reef

Pascua City

Pearl
Beach

Rowan Reef Point

Pascua Bay

Uva Point

Southern Beach

Great Richard Barrier

CHAPTER ONE

From the air, the island was exactly as Amy had described it. In the afternoon sunlight, the foam-edged beaches and lush forests of the interior were hostages to the long Pacific rollers sweeping in from the east. Amy had described the Pascua Archipelago as a group of eight islands stretching across a hundred miles of ocean. Only two were inhabited, Pascua and Pascua Petit. This did not include Crab Island, the one her father owned; the size of six small hockey fields she had added laughingly. Located five miles to the west of Pascua, it was a useful haven for their vacations.

The plane tilted slightly and, for a heart-stopping moment, a mountain reared up ahead of them. Then as the Viscount banked in a slow turn to line up with Pascua City airport, the mountain slid away under the starboard wing.

The city appeared unexpectedly from behind the peaks of Hungry Mountain, revealing a breathtaking view of a city that could have been designed by a mathematician; roads intersecting at exactly ninety degrees, and building plots as uniform as squares on a chessboard. Abruptly the symmetry was broken as the business district appeared under the wings. Brick and iron warehouses were tucked away amongst tall buildings with steep mansard roofs that reflected the nineteenth-century French influence. Yet the name, Pascua, suggested an Italian connection somewhere.

I'm desperately afraid, Amy Carter had written. *I don't know what to do any more. Someone will die. I know it! I can feel it! Oh God, if only I could find someone to help me. Someone I can trust. Daddy is so wrapped up in his bloody theatre; if I told him he wouldn't believe me anyway.*

I can't believe it either, Emma thought morosely. I can't believe I dropped everything and caught the first plane out. First flight from South Africa to Sydney, and the first Island Hopper Line to Pascua. It wasn't as though Amy had asked her to come, but Emma had interpreted the letter as a desperate cry for help. So here she was, and Amy didn't even know yet that she was on the island. She would phone the Carter home from the airport.

Her husband, Teig Olsen, had been incredulous. 'Don't be so damned quixotic. What on earth do you think you can do?'

'I don't know,' she had said stubbornly. 'Probably nothing, but I have to go. She was my best friend at school.'

'She was an exchange student, for heaven's

sake. She was at Aliwal Park for less than a year.' He made an exasperated gesture. 'And she's visited—at the most—three times in ten years.'

Her reply was a stubborn shake of the head. 'It was enough. We made promises. I at least have to keep them.'

He had agreed finally, but only on condition that Mack accompanied her. 'I can't go with you. I have a farm to run.' Mack was Colin McGlashan, her husband's stepfather. A tough, formidable former private detective, he had been hired by her grandfather fifteen years ago when they were threatened with the loss of Cold Water Farm. He had stayed on and married Ursula, Teig's mother.

The thump of the lowered undercarriage drew her out of her reverie. She looked down to see the ground rushing past and the runway coming up to meet them. Next to her, Mack was in the aisle seat, his eyes closed, his hands clutching the arm-rests. He hated flying.

*　　　*　　　*

The airport lounge was small but equipped with every modern facility for handling the hundreds of tourists arriving on the daily flights from Sydney and Los Angeles. There was a comfortable bar and restaurant, and an efficient customs gate manned by courteous men and women, most of whom appeared to be Polynesian. The décor was pale-yellow; pale-yellow floor tiles embossed with geometric shapes in a pale fawn, were matched with curtains of the same shades of yellow and fawn. Emma wrinkled her nose. Doesn't do much for the hothouse ambience, she thought moodily.

Windows on three sides gave a clear view of the service road and car-park. Beyond the car-park was a grove of the ubiquitous palm-trees that appeared to have been planted by a tourist-board to impress visitors, and to remind them that they were on an island in the Pacific. Beyond the trees however, a busy highway emphasized the metropolitan nature of the island.

While Mac waited for their bags she walked to the window. The hot sky above was burnt to a blue-white glare that was nothing like the cool colours of the travel-office posters. A heat-haze hung over the car-park and small mirages shimmered on the hot tarmac. Between the car-park and the palm-trees were colourful flower-beds, while red hibiscus and yellow frangipani alternated at the edges of the lawns. It was all too painfully formal, as though one of the undergardeners had been told to pretty up the airport perimeter.

Emma walked to a bank of telephones near the restaurant entrance, took a silver piece from her purse and wondered if the unfamiliar coin would be sufficient. She shrugged and picked up the receiver.

Most of the travellers had drifted out into the car-park to be driven away. Homeward-bound tourists flying out on the next plane began to drift in from the car-park.

Snatches of conversation reached her at the call-box.

A plump woman in a white sun-suit. 'The chef should have been shot. I'll never look at roast pork again in my lifetime.'

'We should be home by ten.' This from an elderly man to his elderly wife.

Disconnected scraps emerged from a group of teenagers struggling with camping gear.

'With a boat like that . . .'

'A millionaire if ever I saw one.'

'I was looking at the daughter.' Confused laughter followed them to the information desk.

A stunningly beautiful woman in a pale-blue sun-dress hurried ahead of her mousy companion. 'I'll get those bloody negatives if it's the last thing I do.' She sounded desperate. Emma watched the woman striding angrily across the crowded hall, sensing fear beneath the woman's desperation. Emma felt a momentary frisson. Turning abruptly to look for Mack's comforting bulk, she was aware of a sense of relief at finding him at the carousel.

Mack picked up their bags and dumped them into a trolley. He wasn't a tall man, but his body was trim and muscled. At fifty-five, his salt-and-pepper hair was still as thick as it had been when he was thirty. He wore fawn drill trousers and a plain light-green shirt. His shoes were brown moccasins, a style he had favoured since leaving the armed forces.

He looked across at the girl. She was standing near the restaurant with her back to him in a pose he knew well. Her arms were folded, her head held high and her feet apart. It was her unconscious response to a moment of decision, after which she would relax and nod slightly. She did that now.

She was as determined as she had been at eight years of age when he had first seen her at Cold Water Farm. Even at that age she was bright and quick, with the ability to see through equivocation or sophistry. She was pretty then, and she was beautiful now. She was fiercely loyal to her friends, and it was this loyalty that drove her to leave her lovely home on the banks of the Tugela River in South Africa to come half-way around the world because a friend needed her.

She was her grandfather's disciple, and it was evident to anyone who saw them together that the bond between them was forged in love and respect. Since Robert Delancy was a widower, and Emma's parents had died when she was a baby, it was not surprising that they were so close.

Even when she married, the bonds were not loosened. How could they be when her

6

emotional ties to each of the men in her life were totally different? The one complemented the other since Teig's devotion to her grandfather was equally strong.

Abruptly she turned and walked quickly towards him. 'The housekeeper answered. She wouldn't give me any information except to say I should ring after five.' Her brow wrinkled. 'I've a good mind to go out there.'

Mack looked longingly towards the restaurant. 'Not before we have lunch.'

She nodded and smiled. 'Never short of a good idea, are you Mack?'

She led the way towards the restaurant.

CHAPTER TWO

It always seemed to Blaine Carter as if the car slowed of its own volition at the last bend before the mountain came into view. It was almost as though it was seized by a conditioned reflex, a sort of Pavlovian reluctance to ascend the final slope to the house on the hill. It was silly of course, merely an illusion he had fostered to assuage the inevitable guilt he felt at his own reluctance to arrive at the entrance gate beyond the trees.

It was a beautiful house in a beautiful setting. From a pair of wrought-iron gates which opened automatically at the touch of a remote-control button, the gravel drive swept in a gentle curve past manicured lawns and tulip beds to a cluster of buildings enclosed within white-painted post-and-rail fences. There were stables, garages with servants' quarters above them, a workshop and the house itself, a low ranch-style building containing seven bedrooms, four bathrooms, a lounge, drawing-room and his own study. The property came with a hundred acres of fertile grazing for the horses, while above all this pastoral amity, Hungry Mountain soared in craggy splendour.

Even though he had paid for the house, it would be a mistake to believe that it belonged to him, since his second wife Juliet had claimed a sort of specious title by right of overweening rapaciousness. This was of no consequence to Carter. Beautiful and comfortable though it was, he had long since regarded his home as an imitation of every glossy reproduction in *House and Garden*; an architectural cliché. He did not dislike the house. Indeed, there were times when he savoured its comfort. His aversion was merely a reflection of the way he felt about Juliet.

Eighteen years ago, just before they were married, she had brought him to view the house and such was his overwhelming fascination with her that he had laughingly paid the exorbitant asking price. He did not even know at the time how much he had paid

8

for it since he had inherited his father's wealth, his extravagance and his beneficence. His first wife had died when Amy was three, and he had agreed with Juliet that this would be the right place to raise his child.

He stopped the car a hundred yards from the gate just out of sight of the house. From behind him the rays of the late afternoon sun gilded the mountain with a molten glow, while the tops of the trees on the slopes of the foothills were touched with the same, though more delicate, shade of gold.

A stork flapped and glided into the pasture behind the stables while in the trees alongside the road weavers called and quarrelled as they began to settle into their nests. The woods were a haven for hundreds of birds. His daughter Amy, in her brief birdwatching period, had counted about thirty species within half a mile of the house.

He remembered how in the beginning he would hurry home from the theatre, the tensions of a day's rehearsal slowly ebbing away as every mile brought him closer to this seemingly tranquil Eden. Then over the years as the tensions of the theatre began to pale before those developing at home, he found himself more and more reluctant to face the endless series of verbal brawls that littered the remnants of their marriage.

Slowly he put the car into gear and drove through the gates.

Mrs Garland opened the door for him and took his coat. She had been waiting for him—an ominous sign.

'The Girl is out at the stables.'

Amy had always been 'The Girl' to Mrs Garland, who had been with the family for forty years. She had been sent to his father by an employment agency after his mother had died. Tall and thin, Mrs Garland's forbidding appearance and sharp tongue hid a kind and generous nature. She was devoted to his daughter but he often felt she was overly protective. Mrs Garland still looked upon Amy as a motherless child.

She hung up the coat, closed the door and started for the kitchen.

Carter frowned and loosened his tie as he walked through the hall.

'When did she get back from the office?'

She stopped and looked at him. Her glance was enigmatic.

'At three o'clock.' She turned to go and then hesitated. 'Mrs Carter is in her bedroom.' Her disapproval was obvious. Juliet had been offensive again; an occurrence which was by no means a rarity in this household. He wondered tiredly how serious it was this time.

'Thank you, Mrs Garland.'

He paused in the hall to straighten the picture hanging over the escritoire on the opposite wall. He loved this painting. It was a superb copy of *The Avenue at Middelharnis* by

10

Hobbema which hung in the National Gallery in London. The clouds and trees soared upwards for three-quarters of the scene, and he always ached to accompany the figure down the avenue to some unknown tomorrow. He sighed deeply, and turned away.

He went through the side door and crossed the lawn towards the stables. The sun was lower now, throwing long shadows towards the east. He smiled ruefully as he recalled that when he first came here he had entertained an agreeable fantasy that the prostrate shadows were paying homage to the magnificence of the mountain above them.

Carter looked up at the summit. From the south end of a short plateau, a conical peak pointed to a clear blue sky, but a faint mist had begun to trail from the pinnacle, a sure sign of rain later. Only the tip of the peak was in sunlight now. This was the time of the day he loved most, when the green of the pasture was darkening, the trees were hiding their foliage in the shadows and approaching night cooled the crisp clean air.

As he turned into the stable yard, six heads turned as one as the horses peered curiously over the half-doors. The sweet pervasive odour of horses, new hay and oats filled the air. He stopped at the first stall to savour this rare moment of pleasure.

The sound of voices raised in anger came from the office at the other end of the yard.

Then a girl stormed out of the office and left the yard, walking swiftly towards the apartment stairs. She was the same age as his own daughter but Carter's unbidden thought was that his daughter was more discreet in her application of lipstick, blush and eye-shadow.

Harry Martin, Carter's stable-manager, came from his office, pausing when he saw his employer. He shrugged uncomfortably.

'No accounting for the young nowadays. Wild and restless, but Sylvia's no worse nor better than most. Thought she'd settle down when she married Les.' He lifted his hand in exasperation. 'Only home for two weeks and still finds time to mix with the wrong lot.' He took a deep breath and smiled. 'Easier caring for the four-legged ones. Her vacation ends tomorrow. Can't say I'll be sorry to see her catch that plane. Been hard for her mother too.' He turned and closed the office door, locking it after him. He nodded towards the end box. 'A bit of tooth problem there. I'll see to it in the morning. The lads have left already.' He had two grooms to help him. His wife Gerda, a veterinarian, was responsible for the health of the animals. She was an accomplished horsewoman, with a good seat and strong sensitive hands.

Harry paused. 'I wonder if I might go over to your island for a quiet picnic?'

'Of course, Harry. Any time. You know that.'

'Thanks, Blaine. It does both Gerda and me a power of good to get away for a day. Every time we go there, I swear it adds a year to my life.'

Blaine smiled. 'I must be working you too hard.' He paused. 'All well otherwise?'

Harry nodded, ran his hand over his bald pate and inclined his head towards the open paddock at the end of the yard. 'No business of mine, Blaine, but you'll need to see to the problem out there.'

Carter put his hand on his manager's shoulder. 'Thanks, Harry.'

When he went out to the paddock Amy was standing with her back to him, leaning against the spectators' bench with her elbows on the top rail of the fence. She was dressed in jeans, check shirt and high riding-boots. She didn't hear him coming, and he stood a few paces behind her. She was staring across the trees at the foothills to the west but Carter doubted if she saw anything of the grandeur before her. His heart ached for her. Though she was now twenty-three, she was still his little girl, someone who had shared with him all the pain of his marriage. He had never intentionally drawn her into the sad situation in which he was embroiled, but over the years, Juliet had slowly driven Amy into a partisan role that neither he nor his daughter had sought. As Juliet became more distant, so Amy grew closer to him. She was a lovely girl, bright, with

13

a smile that some would have described as luminous. She wasn't smiling now.

There was so much ambivalence about his feelings towards Juliet. How does one apportion blame? There were so many questions, so many uncertainties.

As he watched his daughter, a small breeze twitched a tendril of her auburn hair, and as she brushed it away from her face and turned her head slightly, he knew she had sensed his presence.

'Mrs Garland told me you came home at three o'clock.'

She nodded, but remained with her back to him. 'I finished up early. James told me I needn't stay.' James Riley was some sort of bureaucrat, a class Carter never understood. All he knew about the government was that it relieved him of more than half his income each year, and that Amy had a position in one of its many departments, a position that took her across the world from time to time.

There was a long silence. When she spoke her voice was soft. 'Did you see Mother?'

'No. She was in her room.' There was a long pause. 'Is there any reason I should have?'

She shook her head without turning. He walked up close behind her, took her shoulders and turned her gently towards him. Then he saw the bruise on her cheek and the cut over her eye. She looked at him and the tears coursed down her cheeks. She clung to him and buried her head against his shoulder.

'Oh Daddy, I'm so sorry.' Her voice was muffled. 'She accused me of coming home early to spy on her. She said I wanted to see if there was a man in the house.'

He felt a rush of anger. How dare Juliet accuse her daughter of spying? A daughter who wanted nothing more than to win her stepmother's love and respect, but who had been neglected and ignored all her life.

He put his hand under her chin and lifted her face. 'How did this happen?'

She dropped her arms and turned away from him. 'It doesn't matter.' She walked a few paces to the bench and sat down. 'Anyway I was angry and rude.'

'Did you feel you had a right to be?' He went on before she could reply. 'Yes I know I have always insisted that you respect your stepmother, but respect has to be earned.' He walked to the bench and sat next to her. 'And I realize that there are times when the effort becomes too difficult. I understand that, but I cannot condone disrespect.'

She stood up impatiently and turned to face him. He held up his hand before she could speak. 'Neither can I condone her insult to you. I'll speak to her about it.'

She shook her head. 'For God's sake, Daddy.' She turned away angrily. 'Listen to yourself. You sound like a pompous headmistress.' She turned to face him. 'When are you going to come into the real world and make your mind up about her? For years, you have let her betray and humiliate you, and all you did was to stand by and watch her doing it; as though she were doing it to a stranger.' She gestured impatiently. 'For years I've waited for you to act, to take back your life and send her packing.' There was a long pause, then her shoulders slumped as she sat on the bench. 'I'm sorry. I shouldn't have said that.'

Carter was confused. He had never heard Amy so bitter, or so outspoken. It was a measure of her distress that she spoke out so frankly.

'No. You have a right to say what you think.' He stood up and walked to the fence. He spoke without turning. 'I think it's time to face the issues head on.' He turned and looked at her. 'We can't avoid them any longer.' He paused, searching for the right words. 'Early in our marriage, before you were able to understand how bad things were, I shielded you from the awful battles we fought over her behaviour. To her credit, she never quarrelled with me in your presence.' He took a pace towards her. 'Finally I discovered that I no longer cared. However I warned her that if her conduct was intolerable, I would divorce her and she would be penniless. There were to be no more parties at this house; no more invitations to her Country Club friends to meet the cast of my plays. She continued to defy me, knowing I would never see you deprived of a mother for the second time.' He shrugged. 'It wasn't weakness that prevented me from throwing her out.'

'I'm sorry, Daddy.' The light was fading quickly. A faint glow in the west was all that remained of the day. He couldn't tell if she was crying, but there was a shake in her voice. 'I don't know how you have absorbed so much punishment.' She shook her head impatiently. 'I only know I've had enough. I have to get away. I love you, Daddy, but I can't go on knowing you are too tractable to take a stand.' Her voice rose. 'Oh I realize now that you were shielding me, but it has gone beyond that.'

Suddenly Carter felt cold. It wasn't the night. It was the thought that his complaisance over the years had caused her so much unhappiness that she had to leave home to escape it. Tractable? She was right, he thought bitterly. He looked at her.

'You think I've been too weak?' It was dark now, and he couldn't see her face. 'Perhaps I have been, but it was that or violent confrontation.' He paused and waited for her to speak but she remained silent. He went on: 'I wanted to spare you that.' He shrugged. 'Or at least that's what I told myself.' He looked up at the mountain, now a dark mass silhouetted against the luminous night. A horse stamped and snorted in its box. The stable odours were strong in the clean night air.

Carter heard a rustle as Amy shifted uneasily. 'James has offered me an assignment. I came home early to talk to you about it, but this incident with Mother convinced me I should take it.'

When Carter looked back on this moment, he would feel again the sense of deep despair. He had failed his daughter.

'I should have sold the theatre the day my father died. I should have given you more of my time.'

'Daddy, no!' She stood up quickly and put her arms around him. 'You've always been there when I needed you. I loved the times when you took me to watch you work. I don't know any other child who was as lucky as I was.'

He held her tightly for a moment, then kissed the top of her head. 'We'd better go in. I have to be back at the theatre early tonight.'

'I'll call at your office before I leave for the airport.'

He was dumbfounded. 'So soon. You're leaving tonight?'

She wiped her eyes and nodded. 'Ten o'clock. I was hoping to talk to you first.'

'How long will you be away?'

'I don't know. As long as it takes to complete the assignment.'

'How are you going?'

'British Airways.' He waited for her to tell him where she was going, but she remained silent. She never spoke about her work, and he respected her reticence.

The yard was deserted. The boxes were closed but the big overhead floodlight was on. He heard the occasional stamp as the horses settled down for the night. There were lights in the window of the Martins' apartment over the garage. Mrs Garland's quarters adjoining his were in darkness. She generally retired after nine o'clock.

The house was dark when they went in. Amy switched on the hall lights as she went through to her room to pack. Carter heard a clash of pots in the kitchen. Mrs Garland had set a single place at the dining-room table. Carter assumed it was for Juliet. He never ate before leaving for the theatre, preferring a late meal sent up to his office during the last act.

He went through to shower and change. His room was at the opposite end of the house from the one Juliet occupied. There was no sign of her, and he assumed she was still sleeping off whatever had brought about her latest bout of ill-temper.

As the warm water coursed over his body, he felt the tensions of this awful day begin to subside, and by the time he was dressed, and had tied his black bow tie, he felt almost cheerful.

Almost! Amy's decision to leave was a dark

shadow on his buoyant mood. He went into the study and stopped. The desk lamp was on and Juliet was curled up in his big chair by the empty fireplace. She looked up at him with a curious look, almost of defiance, but there was something else there too. If Carter hadn't known it was impossible, he would have said it was an expression of entreaty. He was still angry with her, but there was no time now to confront her with her abominable behaviour towards Amy.

He went to his desk and filled his pockets with the objects he had left there before showering. He went through the ritual mnemonic: *comb, handkerchief, keys, pen, spectacles, wallet.*

Carter looked at her. She was staring into the dark fireplace. She was in her kimono, her black hair still damp at the ends, where the shower cap had not quite reached. He looked down at the desk, taking his time to stow each item, waiting for her to tell him the reason for this unusual call. She never visited him in his study, but although she was volatile and unpredictable, she sometimes surprised him by doing something rational.

He glanced at her. He had to admit that even though she was in her late forties, she was still a beautiful woman. Beautiful, deceitful, selfish and corrupt.

Judgemental? Of course I am, he thought bitterly. He had stayed in a useless marriage for the sake of his child, but Juliet had gone too far and now his child was leaving. What a useless sacrifice it had been!

Carter waited for her to speak. He never initiated a conversation with Juliet. He had learned to his cost that she could be provoked to anger, by even the most innocent remark. She had a highly developed persecution complex.

She looked up at him. 'You look good in that outfit. Distinguished.'

'What? This old thing.' Droll, he thought 'This tux is at least three months old.'

'Tux! God, what an old-fashioned word.'

Carter became defensive. 'I like *old-fashioned.*'

'Dammit Blaine! Of course you like it. It's your security blanket. You do things the way your father did, because you don't have an original thought of your own.'

'Rubbish. I kept whatever he did that worked for me. I modernized the theatre and brought new methods.' For a moment he felt a twinge of disloyalty. He shrugged it off impatiently. My father would have approved, he thought angrily 'I kept up his standards.'

'Of course.' Her tone was mocking. 'Like those deadly old-fashioned plays you put on.'

Carter was stung. 'Those deadly old-fashioned plays are still drawing good houses.'

'Lord, you *are* stuffy. For heaven's sake, Blaine, you are playing to geriatrics who

21

probably still remember seeing Irving.' Her voice rose. 'And most of the tourists probably saw the original Broadway and West End productions. They'll dribble away into their graves before the next decade, and where will you find your audiences then?' She turned her body to face him. 'Get into this century, Blaine. How many young people are in your audiences? Count them in the house tonight.'

He shrugged. 'What does it matter? Speculators are already eyeing the property for development. I may accept the next good offer.' He walked to the door.

'Blaine, wait.' There was a long pause. She put her head in her hands. 'Lord, why do I always want to goad you?' Her voice was soft. 'Even now when I need you, I can't help myself.'

Surprised, he looked down at her. 'Me? You need me? Hell, that's a laugh.'

'Please Blaine, don't ridicule me. Not now.'

Carter realized she was serious. She seemed almost distraught. This then was the reason for her odd demeanour earlier; her look of entreaty when he came into the study. He looked at his watch. 'I'm late. Won't this wait? Until later tonight, perhaps?'

She was silent for a long time. It was quiet in the study. The book-lined walls muffled any sounds from outside. The loudest sound was the ticking of the clock over the fireplace. She looked up for a moment and then nodded. 'I suppose I can wait until then.'

She reached up and clutched his arm. 'Please Blaine. Come home early.' There were tears in her eyes. 'You must help me. I'm in trouble.'

He looked at his watch without noticing the time. He hesitated, but this was one night he had to be at the theatre before the curtain went up. 'I must go, but I'll be home early.'

'Promise. Please promise me Blaine.'

'I promise.'

At that moment he felt strangely sorry for Juliet. It was an odd experience. He hadn't felt anything for his wife in years, and now it seemed as though his invulnerability was in jeopardy. Every instinct told him to reject this cry for help. It was a trick; another of her ploys to strike at him. Then he remembered her expression of entreaty. He decided to hear what she had to say when he returned. He heard a low rumble of thunder as he left the house.

CHAPTER THREE

Intermittent thunder followed him all the way to the city, and as he drove into the theatre parking-lot, the first few drops of rain trickled down the windscreen. By the time he walked through the stage door the downpour was rattling against the high windows of the building's ornate Victorian façade.

It was dark backstage. The curtain was still up and on stage a working-light on a metal stand threw out a weak yellow glow that failed to pierce the gloom of the auditorium.

Carter went through the pass door and up the right aisle to the centre cross-aisle. The rows of seats clothed in their deep-red plush were like dark sentinels. He looked at the stage where Rhoda Larkin's set for *The Long Summer* waited in semi-darkness for the play's characters to breathe ephemeral life into this house by the river. He had seen this set dozens of times, yet each time he looked at it he was filled with an almost sensuous pleasure. Rhoda's design was no slavish copy of Jo Gordon's setting for the original Broadway production. The river was there, the summer-house was there, the porch was there, so too was the scrim which was raised before the opening dialogue, but the house reflected Rhoda's love of dynamic proportions. Carter smiled ruefully when he remembered how he had fought with her over this. He had wanted a quiet set which would contrast with the emotions of the dysfunctional family that lived in this house. She had wanted a set that emphasized those emotions, and she had proved him wrong. She knew what he wanted from the play better than he did himself.

My father would have liked Rhoda, he

thought. Oliver Carter had been a brilliant director who had taught his son well. Oliver knew his limitations as an actor, but, wisely, he directed his huge talents towards writing. In the late thirties, he had had two plays running simultaneously, one on Broadway and the other in the West End of London.

Blaine Carter knew that by today's standards his father would have been labelled old-fashioned. He believed that actors should be schooled in all the fundamentals before learning to act. He believed implicitly too, in acting-area qualities long before the idea gained acceptance, and he continued to believe in the theory long after it had become outmoded. Oliver Carter had been a man of his time, and when his father, Bernard Carter, died and Oliver returned to Pascua to take over the obscure Carter Theatre, it was years before playgoers in London and New York stopped asking: 'Whatever happened to Oliver Carter?'

Rhoda had been with the company now for a decade, and it was she who persuaded Carter to do this difficult Robert Hobart play which he had adapted from a Donald Webster novel. He had not been entirely convinced that his company had the people to fill the roles, but the cast he had chosen had risen to the challenge. It was with a feeling of quiet satisfaction—and yes—of pride too that Carter recalled that the play had run for longer than the original failed Broadway production which had lasted for only eight weeks. Hobart had predicted that this play would be around for years in spite of its original commercial failure. He was right. It had been around for years. Audiences had reacted with almost universal approval.

Carter walked a few paces towards the stage, sat in an aisle seat and looked critically at the sleeping set. He had enjoyed directing this play, perhaps more than most of those he had brought to life on this stage. In the early days of rehearsals he had believed it was because of the quality of the play, but he soon became uncomfortably aware of the many similarities between certain characters in the play and himself. Of course, there was no parallel with their circumstances and his, but there were moments when the dialogue reflected elements and values which kept sending him back to his own experience. At first it was subliminal, but slowly he found his empathy for the characters surfacing into an understanding of his own dysfunctional existence. As he mused on it now, he was filled with a mood of sombre depression.

The house was quiet as only a dark theatre can be. He began to relax. Above him, the moulded red and gold Victorian ceiling disappeared into the darkness above the three great chandeliers. Without the air-conditioning, which waited for the first patrons, the air smelt of dust and furniture polish tainted with the faint vestiges of cigar smoke which remained in the upholstery and carpets from the time before the red NO SMOKING signs went up a decade ago.

Sounds from backstage shook him from his reverie, and all at once Carter remembered why he had come early to the theatre. He got up and went out of the auditorium.

The red-and-gold motif was carried through to the foyer: six sofas and eight easy-chairs were upholstered in a deep-red velvet with gold piping. Blaine went towards the stairs without his customary inspection.

There were three offices in the short passage above the foyer. Behind the first was where the accountant Ray Dickens and his secretary, Donna Perry, wove their magic to make the money numbers add up to fascinating totals. Behind the middle door was a smaller room occupied by Carter's secretary Wendy Borland. Her office led directly into his. Since his door to the passage was permanently bolted, the only entrance to Carter's office was through hers.

Visitors were left in no doubt that this office was her own personal space; it was her domain. Blaine's father had allowed her to redecorate it herself. She had replaced all the heavy, old fashioned furniture with functional pieces in light-coloured wood and bright materials. Oddly enough, in spite of the informal ambience, there was no doubt that this was a place of business. It reflected her cheerful disposition and lively sense of humour, but there was an air of authority there too.

Wendy was a childless widow. She owned a small house in a good neighbourhood but the theatre was her life. When her husband, Jeff Borland, died, she immersed herself in her work, slowly bringing to it all the energy she had hitherto reserved for her beloved companion.

Wendy looked up from her typewriter as Carter entered. A nod of her head towards his office door told him Kenneth Haig was already there. His contract file was in Wendy's OUT tray where she had placed it for Carter's attention. He sat on the edge of her desk and flipped it open. A ten-by-eight publicity still was clipped to the inside page.

Kenneth Haig was tall with an actor's good looks, and at forty his hair showed no signs of grey. He was a passable actor, but spent more time resting than many of his contemporaries. He lacked that indefinable quality that captivated audiences and impressed producers. He was stranded in an outdated, elaborate acting style that directors found difficult to restrain. It was his lack of imagination too, that prevented him from establishing that rapport with his colleagues which is so necessary between actors. His barely concealed derisive attitude towards his fellow actors caused him to be an undisciplined performer. In spite of this Carter had put him on a six-month contract, anticipating some roles for which he was ideally suited. He had been cast in two other roles during this time, but he had worked for the Carter Company several times over the years. His contract expired when *The Long Summer* closed. His part in the play consisted of a long scene in the first act, two small appearances in the third act and almost an hour of rest in the greenroom during act two. He had been reluctant to take the part at first, but faced with the prospect of a long rest, had finally accepted it.

There was a stab of lightning and a crash of thunder, followed by a downpour that rattled against the windows. Wendy got up to close the curtains as another flash of lightning lit up the office. She went back to her typewriter.

Carter looked up from the file to see Wendy watching him. Her face under her short greying hair reflected her disapproval, whether of him or Haig he didn't know.

'I hope you're going to be firm about this, Blaine. Your father would have fired vermin like him in the first week.'

'Oh come, Wendy. He is a little tacky, but vermin—'

She cut him off. 'I said vermin, and that's what he is.' She sighed with exasperation. 'I've seen Oliver Carter getting almost physical with people like him.' She swung her chair back to face the typewriter. 'Now stop being so damned tractable. Get rid of him.' With a dismissive gesture she went back to her keyboard.

He looked at her with astonishment. Tractable? The very word Amy had used to describe him. The depression he had left in the auditorium returned more deeply than ever. He stood up, taking the contract with him.

Blaine Carter's office was large, with a heavy curtain covering the window overlooking the street. The furniture and panelling were of heavy mahogany and dated back to his grandfather's day. Bookshelves which covered the entire wall opposite the window contained copies of every play presented in the Carter Theatre since it had been built nearly a hundred years ago.

Haig was seated in the big armchair with an open copy of *The Remarkable Mr Pennypacker* on his lap. He looked up as Carter entered.

'Well look who's here.' He closed the script and tossed it back on the desk.

'I'm sorry, Haig, I was held up.'

Haig smiled sardonically. 'I glimpsed you snoozing in the auditorium, just now.'

At once Carter's depression was transformed into cold anger, but he maintained an icy calm.

'Indeed. Is that what you think I was doing?

Snoozing?'

'It looked that way to me.'

'Perhaps. If you say so.' He wasn't prepared to debate this childish issue with Haig. In any case, he had been five minutes late and was prepared to allow Haig his small irritation.

Haig gestured to the script at the edge of the desk. 'I hope that isn't the reason for this meeting.' He shook his head. 'Dear me, Blaine, not another old-fashioned offering from a Broadway long gone.' He made a theatrically dismissive gesture. 'I couldn't possibly accept a part in that.'

Old-fashioned? Carter's anger was deepening. 'I didn't ask you here to discuss my plans for the rest of the year. I want to talk about your contract.'

Haig bridled. 'Look here, Blaine. If you're considering a salary cut in my new contract, I won't stand for it.'

Really the man was impossible. Wearily he picked up Haig's contract and placed it carefully in the OUT tray. Whatever lingering thoughts he had had about keeping him on disappeared along with his anger. Even at that late stage Carter paused for a moment, wondering if he was being quite fair in allowing his melancholy to cloud his judgement. This was an important decision that could affect the man's career and perhaps his whole life.

All at once, Carter realized what he was

doing. That tractability, that flaw that prevented him from acting with resolution, was interfering with a normal business decision. He looked up to find Haig regarding him with a curious look. Contempt?

'There's no new contract, Haig.'

Haig's reaction was almost too casual. He knew. He had known all along and the revelation filled Carter with an emotion that was a combination of fury and shame. Was this how others saw him? Weak? Vacillating?

Haig's expression changed to one of boredom. He shrugged. 'I expect something will turn up.'

There was a knock at the door and Wendy entered with the envelope containing the figures for the evening performance.

Haig smiled at her. 'Full house tonight, Wendy? They love me here. I'll be missed.' He stood up and walked to the door. Wendy smiled and raised her eyebrows. She knew Blaine had let the man go.

Suddenly Carter knew why the actor had taken the situation so calmly. He'd had another offer. 'No need to worry, Haig,' he said. 'They'll love you just as much at the Tivoli.'

Haig stopped, a look of chagrin on his face. Then he smiled. 'Give my love to Juliet.' He went out.

Carter looked at Wendy as she placed the envelope in the IN tray. She avoided his eyes, no longer smiling. She walked around the desk towards the door and closed it softly behind her.

Carter sat at his desk, oblivious to the clutter of papers before him. He was stunned by the revelation that he knew less about Juliet's lovers than he'd thought he did and that her shortcomings were common knowledge. Shortcomings? Was that the strongest word he could find to describe her cheap, disreputable betrayal of their marriage, a betrayal that shamed both him and his daughter? At that moment in the midst of his pain, shame and anger, he could only remember the pain Juliet had caused Amy.

It seemed inconceivable that any woman could succumb to a man like Haig, but it was all too clear that she had done so. Haig's transparent behaviour and Wendy's intense dislike of him left Carter in no doubt. Vermin? The epithet had startled him at the time, but now he understood Wendy's abhorrence.

My God, he thought. Shortcomings? In one day he had awakened a truth that he had been suppressing for years; a truth that others had seen and one which had given Amy so much anguish. He had been afraid to face the pain and in refusing had told himself that he did not care, that Juliet no longer meant anything to him, but he had forgotten that Amy's pain must have been far deeper than his. He had always had a remedy if he wanted to take it, but Amy had none. All she could do was wait for her father to take a decisive step, but he had failed her. Even tonight at the stables, he had failed to perceive or understand her anguish. What was it she called him? A pompous headmistress. Blaine Carter's humiliation was complete.

At that moment he longed for her to walk into the office so that he could hold her and tell her how sorry he was. Then he remembered that she was calling at the theatre before she left.

There was a tap at the door. Wendy looked in. 'Curtain up in thirty minutes. Are you going down?'

'No.'

She shut the door and walked over to the desk. 'Are you all right?'

He leaned back and looked at her for a moment. 'You knew about Haig and Juliet.' It wasn't a question.

She frowned. 'Yes, I knew. I hope you're not suggesting I should have done something about it.' She shook her head. 'And if you're going to ask why I didn't tell you, I have no answer.' She paused for a moment. 'Except that I was certain you knew about him. You knew about the others.' She shrugged. 'And the knowledge that you had abandoned any interest in your marriage gave me a kind of escape mechanism for my conscience.' She dropped into the visitor's chair. 'Dammit,

Blaine. If it had been a unique episode I might have told you.' She paused and looked down at her hands. 'I don't know, but I might have.' She looked up at him. 'Anyway it isn't reasonable to expect me to go running to you every time she steps out of line.' Her voice rose. 'And don't talk to me about loyalty.' She stood up, made for the door and turned. 'I watched you watching everything fall apart without lifting a finger. Would it have helped if I had interfered?' She paused. 'Would you have let me?' She opened the door. 'Right now you have a job to do. Get out there and do it. Sitting here feeling sorry for yourself won't solve your problem.' She went out, closing the door softly behind her.

Feeling sorry for himself, he thought. Was that how he felt? He shook his head. That was a nugatory description which trivialized the anguish that both he and Amy had endured.

He stood up, walked to the window and pulled aside the curtain. The rain had eased. Traffic in the street below had thinned to a trickle.

There was a click and sounds from backstage came through the speakers on his desk as the electrician turned on the power to prepare the equipment for the performance. He went to his desk and switched off the speakers. He had no desire to hear Haig's words coming into his office when the play began. His lacerated emotions could not tolerate the sound of the man's voice. He began opening the letters laid out neatly on his blotter. After he had dictated replies to those that had to be answered, he looked dispiritedly at the unpublished scripts sent in by writers who thought their work was good enough for the Carter Theatre.

There was a tap at the door. Blaine felt a rush of irritation, then made an effort to remain composed.

'Come in.'

As the door opened, he heard a buzz of voices as the audience streamed into the foyer for the first interval. The man who entered was tall, thin, and in spite of his obvious youth, was bald. His smile seemed to brighten the room, and with it, Blaine's mood. He liked Culum Garrett. His assistant was a more than competent director in his own right, worked hard and was always cheerful. As he came into the office, his smile became a little strained.

'A small problem, Blaine.' He sat in front of the desk. 'Have you had words with Haig?'

Blaine nodded. 'A few. Why?'

'He's walking through it tonight. Giving nothing to our leading lady. She's furious.'

'I'll talk to Helen. Leave her to me. In the meantime you tell Haig tomorrow that the Tivoli management will be in the stalls some time this week.'

Garret's eyebrows went up. 'Will they?'

Blaine smiled. 'No. But he won't know that.'

Garret laughed. 'Why didn't I think of that?'
'Because I'm more devious than you are.'
'I learn something from you every day.'
'Don't you though.'

*   *   *

The play was well into the second act before he switched on the speakers. He stood up, stretched and looked at his watch. Ten o'clock. He felt a stab of hopelessness. Amy wasn't coming.

His distress drove him from his desk to the window. Behind the half-drawn curtain, the long rain-washed pane mirrored a face that even in the shifting distortions of the wet glass, reflected his misery.

There was a knock at the door.

'Come in.'

All at once, as Rhoda Larkin walked in, the office seemed to be filled with a warmth that dispelled all the wretchedness of the past hour. During all the years that they had been friends Rhoda's presence had always had that effect on his spirits. Her tranquillity seemed to glide under his skin, calming his every turbulent moment. He had never known her to be angry or even irritated.

She was a slim, attractive woman with a smile that was as welcoming as a summer day. She wore her blonde hair short, in the functional fashion of those designers who

37

worked with balsa-wood, papier-mâché, paint and glue where long hair was an impediment. She wore a blue-grey high-collared dress under her white work-smock.

For a moment his concern for Amy, though not diminished, abated somewhat at the thought that Rhoda had news of her, but her first words were not about his daughter.

'Have you thought about the style for *Look For Me Tomorrow*?' She sat in the chair opposite him.

He shook his head. 'I haven't made a decision yet.' He stood up, walked to the window and spoke without turning. 'Why don't you suggest something and see if I like it.'

There was a long pause that stretched into uncomfortable silence. He turned to find her watching him. He shrugged. 'I'm sorry. I'm in no mood for decisions.' He turned back to the window.

Rhoda stood up. 'I'd better go.'

He turned abruptly. 'No. Don't go.' All at once he was embarrassed; not by the entreaty in his voice, but by his seemingly ineffectual retreat from responsibility. He sat at his desk. 'I'll decide on the style tomorrow. I promise.' His attempt at a smile was a rictal absurdity.

'We can talk tomorrow afternoon.' She hesitated, then paced away from the desk towards the bookcase. There was a long silence as she fingered the spines of the play-scripts. When she spoke, her voice was soft.

38

'We've been friends a long time Blaine. Long enough for me to believe that you would trust me if you ever needed a confidante.' She turned to face him. 'If I'm taking a liberty with our friendship, say the word and I'll leave.'

At once, as her words reached out to him, he was overcome by a strange detachment. It was as though his mind had been drained of all emotion. There was no more pain. His anguish was swept away in a tide of quiescence.

'No. It isn't a liberty.' He stood up quickly, breathed deeply and walked to the window. He was touched by her concern. In all her years with the company, this was the first time she had reached out to him on a personal level, and the gesture warmed him.

He heard her move towards him. 'I mean it, Blaine. Call me if ever I can be of help.' She made for the door.

He turned. 'No, wait.' This new side of her was a revelation. It should not have been, given that he had always known her to be gentle and thoughtful. This new dimension drew him into unfamiliar territory, an agreeable state that lifted his spirits and filled him with gratitude. He looked into her eyes for a moment, then took her hand and held it briefly. He saw her colour slightly. He was contrite. 'I'm sorry. I'm just so grateful that you're not only a valued colleague, but also my friend.'

Flustered, she went to the door. 'I'll come in

early tomorrow. Before rehearsal.'

As she opened the door she almost collided with his accountant, Donna Perry. Donna closed the door and looked at Blaine with undisguised curiosity. At forty, Donna was heavily built with greying bobbed hair. She wore a black waistcoat over a white shirt and loose black trousers. Carter wondered why she always went out of her way to accentuate her homosexuality.

He sighed deeply. 'What is it, Donna?'

She dropped a bunch of keys on his desk. 'The safe keys. Ray left early.'

'Oh? He didn't tell me.' Blaine was irritated by Ray Dickens's capricious behaviour. This wasn't the first time.

She shrugged. 'He took a call from Werner Horvitz and rushed out.' Horvitz was Dickens's live-in companion. She went out, closing the door noisily behind her. Carter went back to his desk. By the end of the second act he knew Amy wasn't coming. His brief moment of Rhoda-induced euphoria disappeared in a cloud of depression.

*   *   *

The man stopped his car half a mile from the house at Hungry Mountain, paused for a moment and then drove carefully into the trees until the car was completely hidden. He sat for a moment listening to the night. He breathed the damp scented air of the woods, sniffing it almost as a predator would. Night insects and small animals made their muted sounds all around him. There was no moon. The huge bulk of Hungry Mountain was invisible under black clouds that hovered over the rain-drenched countryside. As he opened the car door, a startled owl flapped noisily in the tree above him. He heard the sounds of its alarmed departure fading into the night. He took a pair of black gloves, two cloth bags and a penlight from the glove compartment, drew on the gloves and stuffed the bags into his pocket. He shut the door quietly and walked through the woods along the perimeter of the grounds until he arrived at the gap in the wall where the original stonework had collapsed. He paused for a moment, looked towards the dark pile of the house and nodded with satisfaction. Only one window glowed behind the curtains. The rest of the house was in darkness. No light showed at the stable or in the servants' apartments.

Moving to a predetermined timetable, he skirted the house, walking softly to the kitchen door, tested the handle and gave a soft grunt as the door opened to his touch. He paused to pull the cloth bags over his shoes, then walked quietly through the kitchen to the dining-room. The thin strip of light under Juliet's closed door went out. He stopped and listened for movement in the silent house. Satisfied that he was the only other person in the house, he went down the short length of passage to the bedrooms. The first was empty, obviously a spare room. Though tidy, the bed was not made up. The next was Amy's; neat, tidy, teddy bear placed precisely between the two pillows on the double bed. He closed the door quietly, went to the right hand passage that led to the study. He opened the door carefully. The sound of a ticking clock seemed to reassure him. A flash of the torch revealed a neat but cluttered room, a single whisky-glass on the desk.

Satisfied, he went unerringly to the room he knew best, turned the handle softly, and heard a faint rustle of a silk garment. He stopped, puzzled, shrugged and went over to the woman in the bed.

A few minutes later he heard the clock in the study chime the half-hour. Pulses racing, and heart pounding, he looked at the luminous dial of his watch. It was 9.30. As he let himself out of the rear entrance, he heard the distant ringing of the telephone.

CHAPTER FOUR

She came out of the rain towards the closed doors of the darkened theatre, walked across the pavement to peer from under the hood of her black mackintosh, looking for signs of life behind the bright reflection of the street lamp in the glass. Blaine Carter took an instinctive pace back into the shadows. The show was over, everyone had left, he was tired, and this was not the time to ask what a young woman was doing in this deserted street at this time of night. The two ends of his bow tie hung loosely from his collar like two threads of weariness to match the threads on either side of his down-turned mouth.

He watched the girl as she walked up the steps, cupped her hands on either side of her face and pressed her nose to the glass. Then she saw him and tapped urgently on the door with her knuckles. The sound was loud in the empty foyer.

Blaine stood quite still, looking beyond the girl at the silent street. It was deserted except for a solitary car parked with its lights out at the opposite kerb a hundred yards from the theatre. He ignored the girl's incessant knocking, watching the car in the rain-washed street. It was a late model Mercedes, dark blue or black; he couldn't tell in the light of the street lamps. The gusting wind picked up a page of newspaper which fluttered across the road and pasted itself against the rear door of the car. Then he saw movement behind the windscreen.

There were no houses in this street, no hotels or restaurants, only the locked doors of the shops that kept daylight hours. She must have come in the car now waiting across the street.

As the incessant tapping on the door continued, he looked at the girl. He shook his head. 'We're closed.'

He heard her voice, muted by the thick glass. 'I'm stranded. I have to make a phonecall.'

He unlocked the door and opened it to the limit of the chain wrapped around the crash bare. 'Pass me your purse.'

'My purse? Why?'

'Just do it.'

She held up the sequinned evening bag. 'It's empty.'

'Humour me.' The girl's slight hesitation and bewildered frown irritated him. He sensed an inherent honesty about this girl, yet she displayed all the signs of uncomfortable equivocation. His years as a director had made him sensitive to all aspects of the human condition including body language and vocal dishonesty. This girl was lying, and her disquiet at having to do so was palpable. His irritation was part weariness, but he admitted to himself that part of his annoyance was caused by her juvenile prevarication which he considered an insult to his intelligence.

'Give me your purse or go away.' He continued watching the car across the street. The girl shrugged and passed the purse

44

through the gap. Blaine closed the door, locked it and opened the purse; lipstick and powder, a few coins, a small pack of tissues and a key on a Pascua Beach Hotel ring. Blaine felt a little foolish. What was he looking for? Deadly weapons? Certainly not in this small purse.

He unlocked the chain, opened the door and handing her the purse, allowed the girl to slip through the gap. He closed the door and locked it, turning to face the girl as she threw back the hood of her mackintosh and shook her hair. She looked up to see him regarding her with surprise. She was more lovely than he'd anticipated, with eyes that reflected the kind of spiritual strength that is achieved only by those who choose unflinchingly the path of probity Her eyes, framed by her well-groomed hair, were the most beautiful he had ever seen.

She frowned. 'What's the matter?'

'Who is your friend across the road?'

She glanced back at the car and shrugged. 'Just someone who gave me a ride from a party.' He heard a trace of some indefinable accent, almost but not quite Australian; and there was something vaguely familiar about her.

'Why didn't he take you back to your hotel? It's no more than half a mile away. Why did he bring you here?'

'We saw your lights go out. He suggested

that I telephone from here.'

'Give me the number. I'll make the call for you.'

The girl frowned. 'I don't know the number. I'll have to look it up in the directory.'

'I'll look it up for you.'

She hesitated. While he waited for her reply, he looked across the road. The car stood there, silently immobile, rain streaming down the windscreen. He looked at the girl. She was biting her lip. In spite of himself he was both intrigued and disturbed by the whole bizarre charade.

He gestured to the box-office. 'There's a telephone in there. It's a direct line.' She made no move, but just stood there biting her lip, twisting the purse with both hands, clearly without the faintest idea of what she should do next. Then all at once a long forgotten memory surfaced, bringing with it a mental image of Amy in a school uniform; Amy with her friends at a luncheon he had hosted for them at a hotel in a city on the other side of the world. What was this girl's name? Emily? No. Emma. That was it.

'You're Amy's friend Emma. Emma Delaney.'

He took her arm and walked her to a sofa. She sat and then looked up at him, her smile a blend of guilt and relief.

'You have a good memory. It was a long time ago.'

He said drily, 'My profession does that to one.' He sat next to her. 'Now tell me what this is all about.' He smiled. 'You're not very good at dissimulation are you?' He thought for a moment. 'I'm sorry. Dissimulation means . . .'

She pouted. 'I know what it means.' She shook her head. 'No, I suppose I'm not very good at it.'

'No.' He stood up. 'But before you begin what I suspect is a very long story, don't you think you ought to bring in your partner in crime? I'm sure he's worried about you.'

*   *   *

Blaine Carter paused in the doorway of the greenroom and stared morosely at the large portrait of his grandfather hanging over the mantelpiece. The air was still tainted with the odour of Haig's cigars. He usually retreated to this place during the entire second act, dozing in the high-backed chair, invisible in the light of the dim sconces except for an elbow on the arm-rest. The mental picture gave Carter a brief stab of anguish, but he refused to allow himself to be disconcerted by anything that would remove his focus from the matter in hand.

Emma, ever observant, saw the brief pause and placed it mentally in a corner of her mind with impressions she had recorded earlier. Something about this room bothers him, she thought. She looked at the cigarette burns on the worn carpet, the unfashionable though comfortable furniture, the dust on the sconces, the bar with scratched top, and wondered if he was embarrassed by the unkempt appearance of the place. She glanced at him, seeing the drawn features, shadowed in the dim light.

Carter saw the look and smiled ruefully. 'Not the most elegant greenroom,' he said. 'Seeing it with strangers makes me realize that I should have done something about it long ago.'

Emma's brow was furrowed. 'Greenroom?' She gestured to the maroon-and-gold décor.

Carter smiled. 'It's a convention of the theatre. A place where actors relax during a play. It's a greenroom in spite of the colour of the walls.'

He led his guests to some chairs grouped around a small coffee-table. McGlashan walked ahead of him, his brown leather jacket rain-darkened at the shoulders. He sat in the chair which separated Blaine from the girl. Protective? Was that his role in this strange affair, Blaine wondered? All at once, he was aware of the tension in this uncommunicative man. He realized too that McGlashan's pleasant features masked his capacity for violence and his undeniable loyalty to his daughter-in-law. It was a loyalty that would prompt him to take the strongest measures against anyone who wished her harm.

Blaine sat opposite them and sighed. 'I hope this is not going to take long. I have a home to go to.' He held up his hand as Emma was about to speak. 'No. Let us make this short. What are you doing in Pascua City, and why did you approach me as if I were an enemy?'

Emma held out her hand to McGlashan. He took a paper from his pocket and handed it to her; she in turn handed it to Blaine. At once he was aware of the nature of their association. Hers were the hands that guided them, but he was the final arbiter of their intentions.

He looked down at the letter that Amy had written to Emma and as he read, his earlier melancholy returned. This was more than a disagreement with Juliet. This raised demons that he never knew existed. In spite of his vast experience with thespian criminals, his knowledge was confined to the bounds of the proscenium arch. This was no stage performance; this was real life. The triteness of his observation escaped him for the moment. It was all he could do to focus his attention on all the unanswered questions. His face mirrored his anguish. His daughter didn't trust him enough to come to him. She confided in strangers. His hurt was deep, deeper than anything he had ever felt in his life.

He looked up to see Emma regarding him with concern. 'Where is Amy, Mr Carter?'

'I don't know.' His voice was hoarse with

49

emotion. He was near to breaking point. 'For heaven's sake, I don't know. She was supposed to be flying out tonight.'

'Flying out?' Emma's voice rose. She glanced at Mack. 'Where is she going?'

'I don't know exactly. Something to do with the tourist board.'

Mack was astonished. 'Your daughter is leaving the country on some nameless errand for some anonymous organization and you aren't curious enough to ask questions.' Blaine was surprised at the depth and timbre of his voice.

Daddy is so wrapped up in his bloody theatre. Emma felt a stab of pity. Poor Amy. So desperate: so isolated.

'I had no reason to ask her.' He rose from his chair. McGlashan stood up quickly to face him, but Blaine ignored him as he paced to the mantelpiece.

Emma listened to the silent theatre. This place of make-believe held a reality that was like a fog of loneliness, a fog that must have engulfed Amy as she was growing up. Unconsciously Emma compared it with the love her grampa had lavished on her, and the pain of Amy's solitary childhood.

Blaine turned to face them. 'She didn't call. She was supposed to call here before she left. What the hell is going on? Who is going to be killed?' He frowned, suddenly angry. 'And what possessed you to act out this charade?'

He went back to his chair. 'And you.' He looked directly at McGlashan. 'How dare you treat me as though I were a monster? Sit down and stop glaring at me.'

McGlashan sat, his expression a little sheepish, but still wary. 'I'm not going to apologize, Mr Carter. We came to the islands without any idea of who the villains were.' He paused. 'We weren't going to rush in until we knew who Amy was afraid of.'

'Dammit, I'm her father. I love her. She certainly isn't afraid of me.'

Emma spoke quietly. 'Has anything happened to upset her recently?'

Blaine went on as though he hadn't heard her. 'Why didn't she trust me? Why was she afraid? We talked this afternoon about . . .' He stopped, unwilling to divulge details of Amy's disagreement with her mother. He was aware of his guests observing him expectantly. He went on, '. . . about some things that were bothering her, but it was nothing she was afraid of.' He went to the bar, leaned against it and stared with unseeing eyes at the portrait of the founder of the Carter Theatre.

Emma glanced at McGlashan. 'Can you think of anyone who may be in danger?' Blaine knew she was speaking, but the significance of her question failed to penetrate his bewilderment. She repeated the question. He looked at her and then at McGlashan, unaware of who had spoken.

McGlashan said impatiently. 'Well, do you know who may be in danger? Amy?'

'Amy! Good heavens no! Why would she be in danger? Who would want to harm her?'

Emma spoke quietly. 'She's missing, Mr Carter. That is a matter of concern.'

'Missing? Of course she isn't missing. She flew out tonight.'

McGlashan stood up. 'Why don't we check with the airport.'

Accompanied by his guests, Blaine went upstairs to his office.

It was well past midnight before they knew that something was seriously wrong. After an hour on the telephone, the only facts that had emerged were that Amy had not left by air, had not boarded the daily inter-island ferry and that she had not left Pascua in Blaine's pleasurecraft which was moored at Uva Cove, a small-boat basin at the western end of Pascua Bay. The officer at the port captain's office was confident that the *Amyrillis* had not passed Uva Heads, the point from which all small craft were monitored.

Blaine left his desk, stretched and walked to the window. He appeared to have regained control of himself. He stared down at the silent street for a moment, then he turned to face his guests.

'I have to go home. She may have left a message for me there.' He paused for a moment. 'I think you should come too. If there is no word from her, we can map out a strategy to find the answers to all this.' He looked at them expectantly and shrugged. 'Of course, if—that is—if you want.'

Emma nodded. 'We're in this to the finish. Right, Mack?'

He sighed and smiled. 'If you say so.'

Blaine nodded. 'Get your bags from the hotel and come back here. You can follow me to the house.'

Mack said: 'Our bags are still in the car. Miss Vitality here drove us all day trying to locate Amy. Coming here was a last resort.'

*   *   *

At the main gate, Blaine waited until Mack drew up behind him. Mack looked at the house, the stables and the wide lawn. Then he looked up at the mountain and quoted with quiet irony: *'A large income is the best recipe for happiness I ever heard of.'* He looked at Emma who was regarding him questioningly. He smiled wryly. 'Jane Austen.'

Blaine operated the remote, then drove to the front of the house. He looked up at the mountain, now visible against a clear starlit sky. The clouds, drifting swiftly eastwards, were a black line over the horizon. The night air was redolent with the smell of wet earth and horses.

Blaine stepped into the hall and stopped,

shocked at the chaos that confronted him. Escritoire drawers were emptied on to the floor, pictures were askew and books were pulled from the shelves. His first thought was for Amy. He almost ran to her bedroom. The door was ajar, and the room had been ransacked. A glance into the study told him nothing had been touched in there. With his guests following at his heels, he went swiftly to Juliet's room. He stood in the doorway, his senses rocked by the sight that met him. Juliet was lying on her side facing him, her eyes staring into his but, unlike his, they would never see again. Carter turned an agonized stare at Mack and sagged against the opposite wall. Mack took a pace into the room, saw the broken mirror, a smashed vase and empty drawers on the floor. As he looked around the room he noted a curious anomaly. In contrast to the chaos on the floor, the bed was neat, with the coverlet pulled up to the woman's chin. He wondered if it was significant. He closed the door, locked it and pocketed the key. Then he went to look for a telephone, leaving Emma to help Carter to his room.

CHAPTER FIVE

The relentless ticking of the clock in the study was an hypnotic irritant to the weary occupants who waited for someone to release them from the constraints imposed by officialdom. Eyes drifted incessantly to the clock face whose hands maintained an apparently interminable path through time.

Finally, as the clock struck three, a tall, well-built detective and his slightly less well-built assistant entered with an assurance that is achieved only by those who are capable of success in their field. The big man turned a straight-backed chair to face his audience and sat. His assistant stood, arms folded, at the left of the door.

In many ways, Joe Sivo was a big man. As head and one-third of the Pascua City Serious Crimes Unit, he was a big man in his community, while as a former member of an Australian rugby football club his bulk had taken him to a successful career in the sport. As anyone who knew him could affirm, his heart was as big as both of these attributes.

His antecedents were a strange mixture of Melanesia and Yorkshire. While he had his father's olive complexion, he had the blue eyes and reddish hair of the girl who had come on holiday from Yorkshire and had stayed to marry the dark, handsome man of the islands. It was to be expected therefore that Joe Sivo's speech was an admixture of his mother's vowel sounds with his father's Melanesian inflexions. Neither was it strange that his own wife was a Yorkshire lass who had overstayed her vacation by thirty years. With her innate flair for business and a fascination with tropical fish, she had built a lucrative business with world-wide connections. Joe, however, while proud of her success, believed that fish should live in the reefs and birds in the forests.

They had one son, Sheldon Sivo, who had inherited his mother's business acumen and had established a successful auto-repair facility on the Largo Point Road, five miles from the city centre.

Joe Sivo looked around the room at the five people sitting in various attitudes of fatigue.

'Right. Now that we are rid of the boffins, and the medical examiner is sure Juliet Carter died between a quarter to nine and ten o'clock, I am going to adjourn proceedings until nine—no—ten o'clock tomorrow morning when some detectives will come back here to review your statements with you.' He looked at his watch. 'Make that this morning.' He paused. 'Before you fall into bed, I have a short statement and just one or two more questions.' He massaged his forehead, a gesture that seemed to his listeners as though he had transferred his exhaustion to each one of them.

He looked up. 'Reporters are clamouring for news of this case. The Carters are important people in this community. They have friends in the government and the Prime Minister has given me permission to call on any source in the Republic of Pascua to assist me to clear this up. Under no circumstances will any of you talk to the press.'

He gestured to the man standing near the door. 'This is Sergeant Billy Williams. He has made a careful inspection of the grounds, and while there are signs of a car parked outside the perimeter wall, the rain has all but obliterated any chance of identifying tyre tracks.' He looked glumly at the people in the room. 'Did anyone hear a car at the critical time?' He paused for a moment. 'No?' He sighed. 'I suppose it was too much to hope for.'

'One moment, Inspector.' Gerda Martin, angular features, thin lips, hair drawn back in a severe bun, was to everyone's image of a horsewoman. 'I have to school two pupils and their horses tomorrow—this morning. And I have to check on the animals at the Hunt Club. I won't be available at that time.' She stood up. 'Besides, what can I tell you? I was in bed by nine o'clock. It's all in my statement.' She walked to the door. 'My husband and I will be available at half past two. Come along Harry.' Harry Martin smiled apologetically and shrugged.

57

'One moment, Mrs Martin.' Sivo spoke with corrosive authority. 'Your daughter, Sylvia Phillips. Where is she?'

Gerda's imperious demeanour was flushed away in a moment of consternation. 'Why, Inspector, she's—she's not here.'

'I'm aware of that, Mrs Martin,' he said drily. 'I asked you where she was.'

'She stayed at the Pacific Towers last night. She is flying out this morning.'

'Thank you, Mrs Martin.' He nodded to his subordinate who left the study. 'And she planned to leave Pascua this morning?'

'Yes, Inspector.'

Sivo nodded. He stared at her for a moment. 'On the seven o'clock flight to Sydney.' Another long pause.

Gerda shuffled uncomfortably. 'If that's all, Inspector, I—'

Sivo interrupted her sharply. 'How did she get there?'

'To the hotel?'

Sivo nodded.

'She went by car.'

'At what time?'

'Nine o'clock.'

'So she left five minutes after Amy Carter?'

Gerda bridled. 'If you knew that, why do you ask?'

Sivo ignored the question. 'They were both here at the critical time. They must both be considered suspects. A full-scale search is

58

under way to find Amy Carter.'

Gerda was outraged. 'Rubbish! Sylvia was with me until the moment she left. Sylvia a suspect? It's ridiculous. Her husband is a well-known, respected company director in London.' She sniffed. 'He won't take kindly to this.'

'Mr Phillips will be apprised of the situation. We will keep him informed of developments.' Sivo rubbed his forehead once more. 'And of the reasons for asking her to postpone her flight until further notice.'

Emma listened incredulously to the exchanges. He's way ahead of us, she thought bitterly. But Amy a suspect? She was about to speak when she felt Mack's hand on her wrist. He gave a slight shake of the head.

Gerda looked at Sivo with hatred as she folded her arms defiantly in an almost idiotic parody of a sullen child. There was a long pause, then she dropped her arms and turned to go.

Sivo ignored her and looked at Mrs Garland. 'Do you think Mr Carter will be capable of answering questions in the morning?'

Mrs Garland, stiff and starched, with every hair in place and looking fresh and rested, pursed her lips in doubt. 'I don't know, Inspector. When he collapsed, the doctor gave him a sedative—a strong one—before I put him to bed.'

'Have you any idea where Amy is now?'

'No. She said she was going to the theatre and then to the airport.'

'Do you know if she was to meet anyone?' Mrs Garland shook her head. 'Or why she was leaving the Republic?'

'No. I know it was something to do with Mr James Riley. Her employer.' She frowned. 'I'm worried about her, Inspector.'

Sivo nodded. 'We all are, Mrs Garland.'

Sivo looked at her for a long moment. He said gently: 'What time did you go to your quarters last night?'

'About half past eight. I wanted to wait until Amy left, but she said she had everything she needed and urged me to go to bed. I went in to see if Mrs Carter needed anything, then I went to my apartment.'

'Did you stay there all night?'

'Of course,' she said severely. 'Until one of your men woke me.' She thought for a moment. 'It must have been nearly one o'clock by the time I dressed.'

'Did anything unusual happen last night? Involving Mrs Carter?'

She said quickly. 'I told you, Inspector; I went to bed at half past eight.'

That's not what he asked, Emma thought. She knew the Inspector was aware of that too, but he merely nodded.

'Thank you Mrs Garland. That will be all for now.'

60

'May I clean up the rooms, Inspector?' She sniffed. 'Clean up all that white powder?'

'Yes, of course. All except Mrs Carter's room. That is sealed until further notice.'

As she left the room, he turned his attention to Emma. 'Now, Miss Delaney . . .'

'Mrs Olsen.' It was obvious to Emma that the inspector had already interviewed Mrs Garland.

'I beg your pardon?'

'I am Emma Olsen. Mrs Emma Olsen.' She paused. 'Clearly, Mrs Garland did not know that.'

He gave her an apologetic nod. 'Mrs Olsen. This letter you gave me. From Amy Carter. You say you cannot add anything to what she said in the letter?'

'No, Inspector.'

'You came half-way around the world on the basis of some vague assumptions.' His voice was bland; a neutral scepticism.

'Yes, that is exactly what I did.' Her voice was equally bland, but her fury was evident. She was exhausted and wished she had never heard of Pascua. Then she thought of Amy, and knew she had to co-operate. She said sweetly: 'Amy's vague assumption was remarkably accurate. Don't you agree, Inspector?'

Sivo nodded. 'You're quite right, Mrs Olsen. My apologies for not giving Amy's foresight the weight it deserves.'

Mack listened to the exchange with increasing scepticism. Like hell, he thought. Like hell he didn't give it weight. When he spoke, his voice was soft.

'Was this the only room that was left untouched, Inspector?'

Sivo looked at Mack for a long moment. 'What did you say you did for a living, Mr McGlashan?'

Mack said blandly. 'I'm a bookkeeper.'

Sivo nodded. 'So you said.' He sighed. 'And before that, Mr McGlashan?'

Mack said uncomfortably, 'I was a private detective.'

Sivo nodded, still regarding Mack with an expression of displeasure. At that moment Sergeant Williams returned. 'I hope you will keep in mind that we are the investigating officers in Pascua.'

Mack looked suitably humiliated, but it was clear that Sivo was not deceived. 'Of course, Inspector.'

'Now that we understand one another, I can tell you that two other rooms were not ransacked.'

Mack nodded with satisfaction. 'So the killer probably . . .'

'Probably found what he or she came for and stopped looking.' Sivo shrugged and raised his eyebrows. 'Or he was disturbed and retreated. So it would appear that this was not a simple robbery. Yes, I'm way ahead of you,

Mr McGlashan.' He frowned. 'And that is as far as I will allow you to go. If you have any ideas, bring them to me.' He looked at Emma. 'And that goes for you too, Mrs Olsen.'

'Of course, Inspector.' She hesitated. 'How was Mrs Carter killed, Inspector?'

There was a long pause. He looked at Mack and then back at Emma. He sighed. 'Well, you'll know soon enough. She was strangled. There are signs of a violent struggle. The medical examiner believes the hyoid bone, and the thyroid and cricoid cartilages were damaged. Of course only an autopsy will be able to confirm his view.'

Emma shivered. She wished she hadn't asked. 'May we go now?'

'You are staying here tonight?'

'We are. Mrs Garland was kind enough to prepare rooms for us.

Sivo nodded and stood up. 'Sleep well, Mrs Olsen.' He inclined his head towards Mack. 'Good-night, Mr McGlashan.'

Emma paused at the door of her room. 'What do you think?'

Mack frowned. 'Of him? Sivo?'

'Yes, him.'

'He is a very capable policeman. Highly intelligent.' Mack smiled. 'Don't be fooled by that dumb act he puts on.' He paused and added thoughtfully: 'There's no doubt in my mind the police found a useful tyre track—in spite of what he said.' He smiled. 'He's a smart copper, that one.'

Emma looked pensive. 'That's what I figured. If anyone can find Amy, he can.' She opened her door. 'Good-night Mack.' She paused and her voice deepened in a creditable imitation of the inspector. 'Make that good-morning.'

Mack laughed, shook his head and walked on down the passage.

In the study, Sivo stood up, stretched and walked to the window, parted the curtains and looked out. In a clear sky a full moon capped the peak of the mountain.

'Be a lovely day.' He turned. 'This damned case puts paid to my plans for a day on the reef.'

Williams grinned and opened the door. 'You say that about every case. Yet you still get out there a couple of times a week.'

Sivo smiled and walked out ahead of him.

*　　　*　　　*

Emma woke to the ebullient notes of a cuckoo which seemed to be calling from the end of her bed. For a moment she was disorientated, her subconscious presenting a picture in her mind of the view of the Tugela River from her window at home. She yawned, stretched and turned over to stare at a tray of fresh coffee and croissants not twelve inches from her nose. She sat up quickly, suddenly aware of her surroundings and alarmed that someone had been in her room while she slept. She stood up, wrapped her gown around her, slid her feet into her slippers and padded to the door. She opened it a few inches to see Mrs Garland's white-aproned figure quietly closing Mack's bedroom door.

'Thank you for the tray, Mrs Garland. Is Mack awake?'

'Not yet, dear. You have plenty of time before the inspector arrives.'

'You're very kind. Thank you.'

Mrs Garland hesitated. She smiled. 'Amy talked of you often; about how kind you were to a new girl in a strange country.' Her smile vanished. 'I think she must have missed her family.' She walked a few paces along the passage and stopped. 'I knew you were a good person even before I met you.' She walked away towards the kitchen.

Emma opened the door wide. 'Oh, Mrs Garland. Is Mr Carter awake? How is he?'

'Yes dear. He's awake. Still very shaken up. Of course he would be, poor man. Very worried about Amy: we all are.'

'Do you think he will see me. Before the inspector arrives?'

Mrs Garland nodded. 'I'm certain he'll see you, dear. I'll call you when he's dressed.'

'Something is puzzling me, Mrs Garland. Why were we all interviewed here? Isn't it customary for statements to be taken at police headquarters?'

Mrs Garland looked shocked. 'Mr Carter is an important man in the Republic. People in his household would never be asked to go to headquarters.'

Emma looked suitably chastened. 'Of course. Whatever was I thinking of?'

Mrs Garland went back to the kitchen.

Emma drank the coffee but left the croissants. She looked around the room. It was large, with a wardrobe and dressing-table in dark oak and a writing-desk in the corner. The wallpaper was a floral pattern in pale green with fern fronds sweeping upwards from the panel corners. The window was enormous, giving a breathtaking view of the wooded foothills and the mountain. Teig and Grampa would love this, she thought despondently. She took a deep breath, aware of a looming regret that she had made a perfectly useless gesture in coming here. She pushed away the thought. Amy needed her: needed someone. No. It wasn't a useless gesture at all.

*   *   *

By daylight, with the morning sun just touching the treetops on the mountainside, and with its rays slanting in golden streamers into every hidden nook in rock and forest, melancholy seemed an inappropriate emotion. Or so it appeared to Emma as she stared from

66

the study window at the glowing peak. Not inappropriate, however, if you were a Carter, she remembered guiltily. She sighed, wondering where Amy was at this moment, and if she knew what had happened in this sad house.

'Good morning.' She turned. Blaine Carter, in olive-green slacks and matching shirt, stood in the doorway, pausing as though he was as awed as she was at the view. Then she realized he must have seen it a thousand times from this window. She thought he looked a little more relaxed this morning; almost as though he had come to terms with the events of the previous night. He walked to the big chair.

'Did you sleep well? Everyone sleeps well in this house.'

The unconscious implication unnerved her. She began to speak, hesitated, and wondered for a moment how she should phrase her condolence.

To her relief, he shook his head. 'There's no need,' he said quietly. 'Though I hope your night was more restful than mine.' He leaned back and checked his watch against the clock above the fireplace. 'Mrs Garland will be here with a tray in a few minutes.'

Emma nodded, strangely comfortable in the presence of this man whom she had met only twice before. Was it his innate kindness, she wondered? Or was it, she thought cynically, his thespian ability to be all things to all men? She was suddenly embarrassed, struck by the thought that the night's events had affected her in ways she had not realized. She brushed away her breach of faith. 'I had a wonderful night.' She smiled. 'That is, until I was woken by a noisy cuckoo.'

He laughed. 'That would be Corky.'

'Corky?'

'That's what Amy—' he paused as he remembered; he continued softly, 'Amy christened him. Corky the Cuckoo. She leaves food out for him. I'm afraid he's become a pest.' Another long pause. 'You were very kind to Amy; and she became quite fond of your grandfather. Yours was almost a second home to her.'

'I can understand that. This place has much the same ambience.'

Blaine rose and went to the window. 'Amy spends a lot of time out there on the mountain. She knows all the trails. She often packs her camping gear and stays up there on weekends. When the weather is fine.'

'Now I can understand why she was so enchanted with our farm.' Emma's eyes strayed to the mountain top beyond the trees. 'That summer, and ones she spent with us on holiday, were the most memorable of my life. We were inseparable.'

Blaine smiled. 'In more ways than one, I imagine,' he said drily. 'What was it I heard? *Amy and Emma, the matron's dilemma.*'

68

She laughed sheepishly. 'You heard that too.' She shook her head. 'We must have been mutual catalysts.' Her smile faded. 'We were so young.'

He smiled. 'And now so very old.'

There was a light tap on the open door. They both turned to see Mack looking at them quizzically.

'Am I intruding?'

Blaine said: 'Not at all.' He went back to the big chair. 'Come in. I've been expecting you.' Before he could sit, Mrs Garland entered with a loaded tray. 'I hope you don't mind. I asked Mrs Garland to bring the tray in here.' He took it from her.

When they were seated, Emma looked at Mack for reassurance. She began hesitantly. 'I don't know whether our presence on the island will make things difficult for you; if it does, please say so and we'll make arrangements to leave as soon as the police are through with us.'

Blaine said quickly, 'I assumed you'd stay. I want you to stay.'

Emma stood up and walked to the window. 'I hardly think there is anything useful we can do, but we came because Amy felt she needed us.'

'I hope you won't leave—at least until we know where Amy is. Stay here. In this house.' He frowned. 'Unless the situation makes you uncomfortable.'

Emma assumed he was referring to the murder. 'You're very kind.' She looked at Mack. 'We'd like to stay here.'

Mack nodded. 'It would be more convenient in every way.'

'That's settled then.' Blaine poured tea for them both. He looked at his watch. 'The inspector will be here soon.' He sipped his tea and replaced the cup on the tray. Emma suspected he had served himself to be polite. He looked at Mack. 'Were you good at your job?'

Mack looked puzzled. 'As a bookkeeper?'

'As a private detective.'

Mack shrugged. 'What can I say? I've had a lot of experience.' He paused. 'Did you have something in mind?'

'I want you to find Amy.'

Mack grinned and looked at Emma. 'I think we're a little ahead of you.'

Emma smiled. 'To be frank, Mr Carter, we had already decided that we're going to look for her.' She paused. 'In spite of the inspector.'

Mack said: 'Do you have any ideas?'

Blaine nodded. 'I want you to start by going out to Crab Island. She may have gone there.'

Mack frowned. 'But the port authorities said . . .'

'I know what they said, but if Amy wanted to go there she would find a way.'

All at once Emma was aware that reality had surfaced. Her image of her role in Amy's

70

disappearance was coated with the kind of illusory heroics that only existed in fiction. In her heated imagination, Amy had been abducted, but her father was convinced that she had left home of her own accord.

She said fiercely, 'Amy would have let us know if she left voluntarily. She would have left a note—a letter or something.'

Blaine shook his head. 'According to Gerda, she left shortly before Sylvia, who swears Amy was not at the hotel. We know Amy never booked in; nor did she take up her seat on the flight. I'm certain she is hiding from someone.' He went to his desk and took a paper from a drawer. 'This morning I spent a few minutes on the phone with the Uva Point office.' He held up the paper. 'This is a list of boats that passed Uva Point in the last fourteen hours. Fortunately the storm kept most boats tied up.'

Mack shook his head. 'And they gave the list to you.' He snapped his fingers. 'Just like that.'

'The law requires them to provide information about boats that pass Uva Point.' He handed the paper to Mack.

Mack's voice rose. 'It's the law. Why, for heaven's sake?'

'So that a missing boat can be tracked at once.' He sat. 'All craft are required to provide details of numbers on board, destination and expected time of return.'

Mack looked at Blaine admiringly. 'Now

71

that's a progressive law.'

Blaine smiled wanly. 'We live in a progressive country.'

Mack said: 'What about other bays or lagoons? Can boats launch from any of those?'

'The only other real possibilities are Rowan Bay and Coup d'essal Bay, but the entrances are barred by masses of reefs. Local fishermen launch small flat-bottomed boats but motorized craft would end up on the rocks.'

Only half jokingly, Mack said: 'Are you sure you want us to do this? You appear to have thought this out.' He thought for a moment. 'What about the police? The inspector said they were looking for her.'

'They are, but I want to find her before Sivo's men do.' Blaine shook his head. 'And as desperate as I am to find my daughter, I can't go today. The inspector wants me to go with him to the theatre.' He went to his desk. 'You will need my authority to use the *Amyrillis*. This is a letter to my skipper. I'll arrange for him to meet you at the mooring.'

As he handed the paper to Mack, Emma saw the slight tremor in his hands. She looked at his face, saw the tension lines, the tight jaw and the distress in his eyes. He's grieving for Amy, she thought. Grieving? The thought shocked her. She meant anxious. She wondered if the tensions were getting to her too.

Mack shook his head. 'How will we find

your boat? As we flew over the bay I saw boats by the score. Every resident and his cat must own a boat.'

Blaine nodded. 'Add the tourists.'

'Well then?'

'There's a port office at the entrance to the small-boat basin. They'll point the way.'

'And the skipper will stay aboard?'

Blaine nodded. 'He'll take you.' He scribbled on a memo slip. 'This is my number at the theatre. Telephone me there if you have something to tell me.'

Mack looked thoughtful. 'Have you considered the possibility that she may still be on Pascua—still be holed up somewhere?'

'I have, but we have to start somewhere, and Crab Island seems the most promising place to begin.'

'It's your call. We'll leave as soon as Sivo is finished with us.'

'You don't have to wait for him. When he called this morning he said he had decided to move the investigation to the theatre. He also agreed with me that there's nothing more you can contribute to the investigation.'

Emma smiled. 'He may regret that assumption.'

CHAPTER SIX

After the storm, the day could not have been more tranquil. As they left the house in warm sunshine, Emma was seized by an exhilaration that she hadn't felt since she was a child. Memories of excursions to the seaside and a long voyage to England on the *Edinburgh Castle* surfaced to awaken a sentience that recalled the smell of ozone and fish, warm sand and sun oil. The prospect of a trip on a cabin cruiser to an island she had never seen excited her. Mrs Garland had even packed a picnic basket. Emma had dressed in a flowery summer frock. That, and her chatter made her appear almost childlike. Naturally Mack had ignored the enchantment of the occasion.

Yet beneath Emma's pleasurable anticipation there lurked a melancholy that was the product of her concern for Amy and the gravity of their assignment. She wondered if Mack felt the same ambivalent emotions. She shook her head. Her grandfather had labels for her various quixotic impulses. Miss Vitality, Miss Impulsive and the most frequently used, Miss Inquisitive. On the other hand, Mack's imperturbable calm would never allow him to feel anything other than the desire to see their endeavours come to a satisfying conclusion. She looked at his face as they drove through the tropical woodlands towards Pascua City. He was relaxed, humming a tune she had never heard, but instinctively, she knew he was thinking of his beloved Ursula, Teig's mother.

Emma watched his face as he took the car around the curves of the mountain road with the deftness of a seasoned driver. Then she saw him slow and take several quick glances in the rear-view mirror. She looked back, but they had just negotiated a sharp curve that hid whatever he had seen.

'What is it?'

He glanced at her and shook his head. 'It's nothing.'

*   *   *

They followed the signs that took them through a suburb of neat houses and well-tended gardens. A sign sent them abruptly to an area of light industries and warehouses.

They had no difficulty finding the *Amyrillis*. It was berthed in a favourable position close to the parking lot.

The skipper was a big heavy-set man of about thirty with hair that had the washed-out blond look of someone who had spent his working life in the sun. Blaine had told them he was Swedish. He was sitting on a small bollard next to the cabin cruiser that Blaine had described to them. He was dressed in a pair of Levis, a denim shirt and clean white sneakers. He stood up and put out his hand to Mack.

'I'm called Olaf. Olaf Greeb. You must be Mr Carter's friends.' His engaging grin seemed to be pasted on his face.

Mack nodded. 'We are. I'm Mack, and this is Emma.'

Olaf smiled at Emma and gestured to the boat. 'This is her then. She be ready to go when you are.'

Mack looked at the *Amyrillis* with a critical eye. She appeared to be in excellent condition, about eight metres long with a three-metre beam. The woodwork was varnished to a high gloss, and the chrome gleamed like a silver mirror.

Mack looked at Olaf. 'Who maintains her?'

The smile vanished. 'Of course, me. I have to keep her—you know, shipshape.' He frowned. 'I service Volvo engines and anchor winch and I paint and polish. Mrs Carter, she always inspect everything.' He paused. 'She bring many people to Crab Island. She liked parties, that one.' He shook his head. 'Very sad business. She is always cross, but still a very sad business.' He turned to help Emma across the small gangplank.

The cabin was spacious and comfortable with highly polished tables and soft leather cushions on the benches. Olaf took his seat on the skipper's stool in front of the wheel and

76

instrument panel. A small radar screen was housed below the panel. There were no charts in sight, but Emma presumed they were stowed in the drawer below the radar screen.

Olaf spoke softly into a microphone before turning a key. The sudden roar of the twin Volvos startled her, then the sound dropped to a soft bubbling. The boat began to edge slowly away from the jetty. Once in the main channel Olaf kept the speed to a comfortable ten knots.

Through the windscreen they were able to see three cruise liners berthed at the Pascua Ocean Terminal, while beyond them the sun-glints shifted and danced on the calm sea. Emma looked out of the cabin to where Mack lounged in the stern well. He smiled, and she suspected he was as exhilarated as she was.

As they crossed the bar, the cruiser rocked slightly on the swells riding in from the open sea. Olaf pushed the throttle forward. As the boat began to lift, the temperature in the cabin dropped to a more comfortable level.

Emma looked over her shoulder towards Pearl Beach where a mass of varicoloured umbrellas blossomed on the sandy shore. Beyond the beach a row of luxury hotels lined the mile-long Pearl Drive.

Ahead of them remnants of a thin morning haze floated above the empty sea. Emma guessed that by midday a fleet of pleasure craft would be on the water. She went out to sit in the stern well with Mack. As she looked west, she was aware of a slight tilt in the motion of the boat as Olaf picked a new course to north-east. Then Emma saw it, a dark speck in the distance: Crab Island.

Olaf took a more easterly course and then abruptly swung south. Emma assumed he was navigating a channel through the reefs. As she watched him he pulled the control towards him and the engines lapsed into a quiet rumble. He turned, grinned and pointed downwards. They looked into the clear water to see an octopus drifting with the current. The creature was at least a metre across, but the six babies that followed her were no more than ten centimetres in diameter. As they watched, the family disappeared into the deep.

Emma looked up at Mack and was gratified to see that he was as enchanted as she was. When he looked at her he was beaming.

'Well, if I see nothing else, that was worth the trip.' He waved his thanks to the skipper. Olaf waved and pushed the controls forward.

The approaches to the island were through channels in the shallow reefs, some of which were beginning to emerge with the ebbing tide. Olaf pointed the cruiser at a small jetty on the beach. The long strip of sand was edged by thick bush and shrub, but to the left of the jetty, a hardened path disappeared into the interior of the island.

Olaf pushed a red button on the control

panel, releasing the winch-driven anchor. He switched off the motors and the boat rocked slightly as the wake of its arrival swept in from the channel.

Olaf helped Emma on to the jetty and picked up the picnic hamper.

'Follow me and watch out for the crabs.'

Emma recalled the tiny crabs she had seen on the seashore. 'Is there any reason why we should be careful of them?'

Behind her, Mack pointed an arm over her shoulder. 'I'd say you should be careful of that one.' There at the edge of the trees, three of the biggest crabs she had ever seen glared at them with eyes on long stalks. One, with a leg span of nearly a metre, was dragging a large coconut as it retreated into the bush. The other smaller crabs scuttled after it.

As Emma gave a stifled scream, Mack walked up the sand and peered into the screen of trees.

'What the hell was that?'

Olaf laughed. 'Coconut crabs. They live in burrows in the bushes, but sometimes go in the water. Females alway lay eggs in sea.' He frowned. 'They are not often out in daytime unless food is scarce.'

'What's it doing with the bloody coconut?'

'He eat it.' Olaf shrugged. 'They be called coconut crabs, but many are seen on islands where there are no coconuts.'

All at once Emma was overcome with a

sense of uneasiness. The sight of these primeval creatures was all the more repellent for their existing in this tropical paradise. She shivered. For a moment it appeared as if a cold breeze had touched her skin. She looked along the beach. To their right the sandy strip ended in a grove of dark mangroves growing in a marsh at the edge of the water, hiding—what? Her earlier exhilaration dissolved, leaving a prickle of dread. Recollections of childhood stories with connotations of sinister otherworld creatures surfaced unbidden. Even the octopus family was no longer a charming encounter, but a manifestation of the dangers all around her. Then the sound of the surf pounding the edge of the reef, and the silent sweep of the water as it swirled in the shallows brought her back to reality. She shook off her sombre mood and followed the two men up the beach.

Olaf led the way along a well-trodden path past a stand of seagrape, a few palms, a stunted tamarind-tree and some thick vines. Then the path ended abruptly at the edge of a coconut-grove which had several windfall coconuts lying under the trees. Well-kept lawns fronted an extensive building with a sharp-pitched slate roof but without any other discernible architectural pattern. A wide veranda ran the length of the building with three doors leading to other parts of the house. The standard arrangement of hibiscus, frangipani and bougainvillaea bordered the coconut-grove. The shrubs were as well tended as those they had seen at the airport.

Mack called to Olaf who was about to enter the house. 'Who tends this place? Where is the gardener? Does anyone live here?'

Olaf shook his head. 'Mr Carter has a garden- and cleaning-service come over once a week. No one lives here.'

'Do you have keys to the house?'

'It's not locked.' Olaf opened the front door and stood aside for them to enter.

They walked into a living-room that was furnished almost like a hotel lounge. Comfortable sofas, easy-chairs and small tables were scattered around a room that could have housed several cars. The thick carpet, in royal blue, showed signs of frequent revels. There was a faint smell of liquor and tobacco. Pictures on the walls were all prints of well-known painters. Each was identified by a small silver plate: *Death of Marat* by David, *Dance* by Matisse, *Rape of Europa* by Titian and *Models* by Seurat. In spite of the clash of styles, or perhaps because of it, Emma wondered who had chosen subjects that were all nudes. The thought came unbidden: the house was like an elegant whorehouse. Then with a rush she remembered that Amy was her friend, and was filled with contrition. However, the impression lingered and she decided that neither Blaine nor Amy could have been responsible for the décor.

Passages went off from left and right of the room, and a double door led to another room with a space that appeared to be a small dance-floor. Beyond that was another double door to a patio and a formal garden. In the middle of the lawn stood a statue of Venus, but with arms. Emma smiled at the incongruity of a Venus with arms across a bare bosom; the ultimate bowdlerism.

Emma turned to Olaf. 'What does Mr Carter use the house for?'

Olaf shrugged. 'He not come often. He's not been for over a year. The theatre keep him busy.' He made a wide gesture. 'Big parties all the time. I bring over many people. Friends for Mrs Carter; sometimes people she meet from overseas. Many times acting people come from the theatre at weekends. Mr Carter never comes to parties.'

It was Mack who reminded them of their assignment. 'My guess is that Amy isn't hiding here, but let's look around anyway.'

Suddenly from the other side of the island came the roar of a high-powered motor starting up. Olaf turned and sprinted through the door of the dance-room and out into the garden. He crossed the lawn and disappeared into the trees. Mack followed him, but Emma was too shocked and confused to move. She sank on to a sofa and waited with heart pounding. She heard distant shouts, and then silence. It was a silence that dragged on until it unnerved her.

She hurried out to the garden and into the trees, where she was suddenly surrounded by thick bush, tall gnarled trunks, and vines that twined in evil loops around trees that were hostages to their desire for sunlight. She appeared to be enveloped in an eerie silence. Where were the birds? There should have been bird-calls. She was seized with an almost paralysing dread. Then she heard Olaf and Mack calling one another on the beach, the far-away pounding of the surf beyond the reef and the faint cry of a gull, and her panic subsided. She felt foolish—silly almost—and she started back to the house.

She took a pace and a flash of white drew her to the edge of the path. There, almost hidden under a bush, lay a photograph. A second and a third were caught in the thick screen of leaves. They were postcard-size prints and a brief glance revealed groups of people holding up tumblers and grinning fatuously at the camera. Behind them was the print of *Models* that hung on the wall of the house; this house.

As she looked at the photographs, her thoughts ranged over her mental record of the last twenty-four hours. None of the events appeared to be linked: the murder, Amy's disappearance and the assignment that her employer had given her. Where was she flying to? If Blaine Carter was to be believed he was so unconcerned that he did not even ask her; neither was he curious enough to wonder what she did for Mr James Riley, nor even who he was. Was she mistaken or had Mrs Garland been just a little disapproving when she'd mentioned James Riley?

She walked slowly back to the house.

＊　　　＊　　　＊

Mack watched as the small open boat powered its way on a line parallel to the beach and disappeared around the headland. The stranger wore a woollen balaclava and dark glasses.

Olaf threw up his arms in disgust. 'Another minute and we'd have got him.'

'Who is it? Did you see?'

'No.' Olaf turned and trudged up the beach. 'Whoever it was, he knew a hell of a lot about island.'

'How do you know?'

'He can't beach here unless he know way between beach and the reef. There is only one way to get here.' He pointed. 'From here is zigzag channel to main reef we came through.' He shrugged. 'This island is entirely surrounded by reef and no entrance show on charts.'

'So if you don't know the zigzag channel we came through, you end up on the rocks.'

Olaf grinned. 'Now you know why we don't lock up house.'

Mack looked across the water to the waves foaming on the reef two hundred metres from the beach. Here the water swirled on to the beach. He was reminded of the Mediterranean beaches off Greece and Italy.

He felt the warm sun on his back and as he followed Olaf into the trees where it was cooler and the path was firm under his feet, he decided that although this island appeared to be a personal paradise for the Carter family, he preferred his home on the farm at the other side of the world. He didn't like this place, and he didn't like the house. True to his stolid conservative temperament Mack preferred mundane people and places that did not raise his discomfort level. He was intensely loyal to the Delaneys, but he stubbornly refused to compromise his standards.

He had never met Juliet, and he was sure Emma hadn't either, but he had met Amy several times. He thought Blaine was a decent man, but with an ego as fragile as fine china. In the light of Amy's apparent voluntary disappearance, he considered her irresponsible. He knew he was being judgemental, but if he disliked compromising his standards, he disliked compromising his principles even more.

They found Emma seated on a sofa by the window with a small table in front of her.

Mack pulled up a straight-backed chair and sat opposite her. Olaf went out through the front door.

Emma said: 'Where's he going?'

'To check on the boat.'

'Who was out there?'

'Someone who covered his face.' He frowned. 'According to Olaf, you can beach here only if you are familiar with the channels. It must be someone we know or have seen, or why cover his face?' He picked up one of the photographs. 'What's this?'

'I found them on the path.'

Mack studied the photograph thoughtfully. 'I wonder if our visitor dropped these.' He placed it on the other two prints and stood up. 'If so, it means he was in the house. I'll look around. Coming?'

Without waiting for her, Mack walked swiftly to the passage at the left of the front door. He stopped. 'Come along.'

Emma stood up. 'I'll take this side.'

'Right. Save time that way.'

'Are we still looking for Amy?'

'Waste of time. I suspect she was our erstwhile visitor.'

'I don't believe it. Why would she run away from me?'

'Whoever it was didn't know who was coming. Didn't wait to see.'

There were doors on both sides of the passage. Mack opened the first door on the

86

right. It was a bedroom with the usual bedroom furniture; dressing-table, wardrobes and two single beds. A large mirror was fixed to the wall on the left of the door. There was a lingering smell of liquor and perfume. He opened the wardrobe door, closed it and looked under the bed. Feeling a little foolish, he left the room closing the door behind him. There were three doors on each side. The next five rooms were identical to the first, down to the perfume and liquor odours. In spite of himself, he opened the wardrobes and looked under the beds. At the end of the passage was a row of bathrooms. All this, he thought, was designed by someone whose existence revolved around the high life. He was closing the door of the third bathroom when he heard Emma calling.

He found her in the passage, standing outside the door of the last bedroom.

'Look what I found.' She led the way through to the *en-suite* bathroom. Photographs were scattered about the floor and the bottom of the bath.

A *frisson* gave him gooseflesh. Was this the break they wanted?

'Is this how you found them?'

'I haven't touched them.'

'Have you been in all the bathrooms?'

Emma nodded. 'All the rooms this side were *en-suite*. Nothing in those.'

Mack looked around the room. Except for

the private bathroom it was identical to the ones he had searched. He went out into the passage, and opened the door at the end adjoining the bedroom. It was a large kitchen equipped with two oil stoves, a butcher's block, a large hotel-size *bain-marie* and pots and pans of all descriptions hanging on hooks over a central work table. He went to a light switch on the wall and turned it on. From a distance came the sound of a motor starting up and the lights came up to full brightness. When he turned the switch off the motor stopped. The system was simple. The first switch that was turned on activated the power supply which remained on as long as there was a switch in the ON position anywhere in the house.

Unlike the passage he had searched, there was only one door opposite the bedrooms. He opened it to find a dining-room that ran the entire length of the passage, with a table that could seat twenty guests. A sideboard stood against the wall and a serving-hatch with a lateral sliding cover opened to the kitchen. He went out and closed the door.

In the bathroom, Emma was on her knees gathering up the photographs. He bent to help her. 'We'll need something to carry these away.'

Emma stood up. 'The picnic hamper.'

'Good thinking.'

Emma went through to the bedroom and piled the photographs on the bed. Mack walked around the bedroom, deep in thought. Then he went back to the bathroom and opened the cabinet.

Emma stood in the doorway.

'What are you looking for?'

'Those prints must have been hidden somewhere.'

'Oh, that.' She pointed at the ceiling. 'Up there.'

He looked up to see a ceiling trap. He grinned at her. 'Clever girl.'

She pouted. 'Don't be so patronizing.' Then she smiled. 'Dammit, I'm good.'

'You certainly are.'

'You going up?'

'No damn fear. I might bump into a coconut crab, or something even worse.'

She pulled a face. 'Coward.'

'You know damn well I am.' He looked thoughtful. 'How the devil did he get up there?' He wandered about the room, looked behind the curtain and then opened the wardrobe. He got inside and looked up. 'Ah. What was it Archimedes said?'

'Eureka.'

'I knew that.' He reached over his head and pulled at a barely discernible loop of rope. They heard two loud bangs. Emma rushed into the bathroom.

She looked back at him. 'Dammit, you're good.'

They stood in the doorway looking at the

open trap through which a ladder had descended.

Emma said: 'Now how does it go back?'

'Counter-weights?' He placed a hand under one of the steps, pushed upwards and the ladder slowly disappeared and the trap closed.

Emma looked at Mack expectantly. 'You're not going up?'

'Definitely not.' He went to the bedroom and picked up the prints. 'If we feel the need, we'll come back, but our first priority is to get a list of the boats that passed Uva Point some time before we did.'

With the picnic hamper emptied and the contents consumed, they stowed the photographs in the hamper and the hamper on the boat. Olaf turned his key and they left Crab Island. Neither Emma nor Mack was sorry to leave.

As they skimmed towards Pascua, Mack looked ahead, his eyes thoughtful.

'I've got it. I know what this is all about.'

Emma said: 'Indeed? Do tell.'

CHAPTER SEVEN

Inspector Sivo looked around the greenroom with distaste. What he saw reinforced his long-standing opinion of the theatre; it was a home for misfits and layabouts. Carter was an exception of course. Sivo's opinion was that the man was locked into a family business but given the right opportunity would have been a professional man of some stature.

He had known Blaine Carter for many years, liked him and considered him a man of integrity and great ability. He was saddened that a man of his intellect should choose the theatre as a career. He never considered for one moment that Blaine liked what he was doing.

Blaine sent him tickets occasionally, and since his wife Ethel liked plays, he made an effort to attend. As entertainment, he preferred films. He made no secret of the fact that plays bored him, and therefore he could not conceive of anyone in the theatre really liking the profession.

He paced the room impatiently. Not everyone had arrived, but since the principal characters were present, he wondered if he should begin. Blaine and Rhoda Larkin were sitting together on the sofa by the window. Helen Summers, the Carter Company's leading lady for the current season, sat on a couch seemingly oblivious to everything but the nail she was polishing. Kenneth Haig had adopted a pose by the fireplace and drummed his fingers impatiently on the mantelpiece. Wendy Borland sat on the opposite side of the room, and if he had analysed her body language accurately, she loathed Haig, and displayed an undue interest in Blaine and Rhoda Larkin. Her gaze shifted to them at regular intervals and her covert glances told Sivo that she guessed what he had divined, that Rhoda had more than a platonic interest in her employer. He wasn't sure if it was reciprocated, but with Blaine as vulnerable as he was at this moment, she could have had him on a plate. He shook his head irritably. What a cynical old copper you are, he thought.

Haig? There was no uncertainty in Sivo's mind about him. A real nasty one, someone Sivo would like to get into the interrogation room for an hour or so.

He sighed. The Summers woman was little better. Blonde and forty-ish with a figure that would be the envy of a girl half her age, she was extraordinarily talented, but she was aware of her value to the Carter Company and exploited it shamelessly. He wondered what had brought her to the island when she could have been in a first-rate company in England or the United States. Admittedly, Blaine Carter's company had a reputation that encouraged tourists to include his productions in their itinerary, but Sivo wasn't all that convinced that it was the high salaries Carter paid his artists that brought them to Pascua.

He studied her surreptitiously for a moment. There were no discernible lines under her make-up and he could see no evidence of surgery. She appeared to be a thoroughly nice person, but he knew that under that façade was a vicious, scheming, heartless woman.

He heard footsteps in the passage. Sergeant Williams, looking a little weary, entered the greenroom holding an official blue-covered Pascua Police Department folder. Behind him was a well-built, handsome man of about forty, with neat black hair that waved very slightly above his forehead. He was casually dressed in a colourful shirt, grey trousers and black shoes. The man moved quietly to a chair by the door and looked at the occupants with undisguised interest. He nodded to Carter who lifted a hand in greeting. Sivo looked at him enquiringly, his eyebrows raised. The man gave a slight nod. Williams took up a position at the left of the door.

A few seconds later Ray Dickens bustled in followed by his secretary, Donna Perry, who was dressed in her customary black waistcoat and loose black slacks. Dickens was his usual oleaginous self, smiling with his lips, his eyes as cold as a glacial wind. He wore a summer suit and black high-heeled boots. He flashed a toothy smile at the inspector, who nodded coldly, and looked ostentatiously at his watch.

'You're late.'

'Dear me, Inspector, surely you didn't expect me at the crack of dawn.' He settled himself at the fireplace, making room on the sofa for his secretary.

'Perhaps you would prefer an interview this afternoon—in my office.'

Dickens subsided with a wide smile, but Sivo knew he had hit a nerve. A previous interview in Sivo's office, following a serious driving-offence, had proved most uncomfortable for Dickens.

Sivo glanced around the room taking a long deliberate look at each of the staff of the Carter Theatre. He wondered if he had been wise to exclude Amy Carter's two friends from this discussion. While they had nothing to contribute to the investigation, bringing them to the theatre might have caged them for a while. They could be the catalyst for complicating his nice straightforward investigation. That man McGlashan was a wily one, but it was the girl who worried him. She was as smart as a rocket scientist, and the pair could muddy the waters if they weren't kept in check. He wondered uneasily where they were at this moment. Up to no good, I'll be bound, he thought morosely.

He turned his attention to his captive audience. 'Now that you are all here—'

Dickens said: 'Not all, Inspector. Anne James isn't here. Our inadequate little *ingénue* is missing.'

Carter frowned. 'Inadequate, Ray?' His tone was cutting. 'Anne is one of the best young actresses we have employed in several years. I suggest you—'

94

'I apologize, Blaine. It's just that she is in such distinguished company—'

'Amongst whom she has shown what a fine actress she is.'

Sivo interrupted the exchanges. 'Miss James is not required at this time, and Mr Carter has confirmed that Mr Garret's duties precluded him from leaving the theatre the whole of last evening.'

'What about my duties, Inspector?' Helen Summers' well-modulated objection drew his attention. 'I was in a play, remember.'

The inspector inclined his head. 'You were Miss Summers, but for thirty-seven minutes you were off stage during the second act.'

'Oh dear. Am I a suspect then?'

'Not necessarily, but you may be able to throw some light on where others in the cast were at the critical time.'

'I assure you, Inspector, I take very little interest in other people when I am off stage.' She paused. 'Unless it's the girl with my lemon tea.'

Her derision left him unmoved.

'There, you see, Miss Summers. You can tell us exactly when you saw the tea-girl.' He made an expansive gesture. 'You can give her an alibi. More important, she can give you one.'

Helen Summers frowned. She had been bested and she knew it.

'You see how complicated my job is, Miss Summers.' He paused. 'Before I was

95

interrupted, I was about to introduce the director of the Pascua Tourist Board, Mr James Riley.' He looked at the stranger as he spoke. Riley acknowledged the introduction with a slight nod.

The inspector continued: 'He is also the head of tourist security. He is concerned about the effect that this murder may have on our tourist industry, and is taking a passive interest in the investigation.' He looked over the assembly and took a notebook from his pocket. 'I'll begin with you, Mr Haig. You are not on stage from'—he looked down at his notes—'five minutes after nine to ten minutes after ten. Where were you during that time?'

'Right here, Inspector. In that very chair with my feet up on that little table. I prefer it to my dressing-room. At least here I remain completely undisturbed until the audience has the privilege of my third-act entrance.'

'Did anyone see you here? Did you speak to anyone?'

'I don't know. My back was to the door. I doze in that chair every night during my break.'

'I saw him, Inspector,' Donna Perry said quietly. 'I popped my head in looking for Annette—the tea-girl.'

'So you saw Mr Haig in here? When you—how did you put it—popped your head in. How did you know anyone was in here if he was sitting in a high-backed chair facing the

96

fireplace?'

'I could see his arm and elbow over the side of the chair.'

The inspector was nothing if not patient. 'How did you know it was Mr Haig?'

'He was wearing that ghastly blue-and-white striped shirt he has on for the third act.' She paused and smiled. 'There was a cloud of cigar smoke over his head. I'd recognize the stink of those awful cigars anywhere.'

'What time was that?'

'Just on half past nine. I had taken the safe keys in to Mr Carter before I went looking for Helen—Miss Summers.'

Sivo looked at Sergeant Williams, gave a brief nod and Williams put the blue file on the small table beside his superior. Sivo picked it up and searched through it briefly. He looked at Rhoda Larkin.

'You left the theatre at nine forty-five. Who did you see or speak to during the period from nine o'clock to ten o'clock?'

Rhoda thought for a moment. 'I was in my office until ten past nine, then I went to see Mr Carter at nine-fifteen. Then about nine-twenty, Donna arrived and I left. I stopped to chat to Wendy for a moment, and then went to my office. I left the theatre at a quarter to ten.'

Sivo turned to Wendy Borland. 'And your movements, Mrs Borland?'

'All of the above.'

'I beg your pardon?'

She smiled. 'I mean I agree with all the accounts you have heard so far. I saw them all at the times they stated, and they saw me. I had a few words with each one of them.' She shrugged. 'After Donna left I went in to see Blaine and then went home. That was about a quarter to ten.'

Sivo looked at Dickens enquiringly. The man shrugged. 'I'm sorry, Inspector, I can't satisfy your curiosity about my whereabouts. I received a message to meet my friend Werner Horvitz at our apartment. When I arrived at nine-fifteen, he had passed out. I put him to bed, read the papers and retired for the night. That was at eleven o'clock.'

Sivo said drily: 'It isn't only my curiosity you must satisfy, Dickens. It may even be a court of law.'

Dickens leaned back. 'What can I say? If I'd known Juliet Carter was going to be killed, I would have made arrangements to be in the company of a hundred people.'

The inspector was equally sardonic. 'I've no doubt you would have cooked up something suitable.'

'I'm afraid you'll have to look elsewhere for your killer, Inspector.'

'But I rang you at home at twenty minutes to ten, Ray.' Donna Perry's masculine voice was emphatic. 'Don't you remember?'

Dickens said suavely. 'Of course. For a moment I forgot.'

Sivo stared at him for a moment, and then turned his gaze to Donna. Then he looked at Carter. 'I think we're done here for the present, Blaine.' He gestured to his subordinate. 'Sergeant Williams will call if we need to take supplementary statements.'

*   *   *

Sivo looked westwards across Pascua Bay from the window of his office on the fourth floor of the Justice Building. As a man of the islands, he loved this particular island and his empathy for his homeland was so deep that it pained him that felons existed in his personal paradise. As a corollary he wondered how anyone living here could consider murder as the solution to a problem.

He swivelled his chair and looked at Williams sitting opposite him, reading over his report.

'Finished?'

'Just about, sir. Only . . .' he paused thoughtfully. 'One thing bothers me.'

Sivo raised his eyebrows. 'Only one? Everything about the case bothers me.' He waited expectantly. 'Well, go on.'

'How can we be sure that it was Haig's sleeve that Perry saw in the greenroom? The girl admits she never saw his face.'

Sivo smiled. 'Go on.'

'What if two people were involved and

99

someone was impersonating Haig to give him an alibi.'

Sivo continued his role as devil's advocate, a role both men appreciated. The inspector once remarked that it kept Williams on his toes. 'You don't think it was too risky? Someone might have looked for Haig and found someone else in Haig's second-act costume.'

'Unlikely, sir. Haig told us himself that in the greenroom he could remain undisturbed.'

'Good lad. I think the possibility is remote, but we should keep it in mind.' He paused. 'Who do you suggest is his co-conspirator?'

'Amongst the staff?'

Sivo nodded.

'What about Dickens, Inspector?'

'Now the stock question. Do you think he is a real suspect, or do you just want him to be?'

Williams grinned. 'I can't bear the oily little sod, and he's the only one without an alibi.'

'Without an alibi?' The inspector feigned surprise. 'But you forget Perry says she rang him at home just after nine-forty. He has a cast-iron alibi.'

Williams said scornfully. 'As an alibi it's about as useful as a hairnet to a bald man.'

'Right. Now let's consider the timetable.' Sivo picked up his notebook from the desk, opened it and handed it to Williams.

Williams read aloud. 'Nine p.m: Garret visits Carter. Stays ten minutes. Nine-fifteen: Rhoda Larkin arrives. Stays until Donna Perry comes with the safe key at nine-twenty-five. Nine-twenty-six: Perry leaves and goes to greenroom at nine-thirty, where she sees what she believes to be Haig's arm, and smells his cigar.'

Williams looked up at Sivo. 'If we believe Perry, then we can write off everybody at the theatre as suspects.'

'Makes our task a little easier. But only slightly.' He turned his chair to the window. Williams waited for the inspector to speak but Sivo watched the bay, his eyes on a yacht moving swiftly past Uva Point. The sun was high and the water looked an inviting blue. It isn't really blue, he thought dispiritedly, only translucent if you looked down into it from a boat deck, but the Lord has allowed us our illusions to make a sometimes murky world a little brighter.

He spoke without turning, his voice soft. 'I am really anxious about Amy Carter. I shouldn't let it become personal, but I've known her since she was a child.'

Williams frowned. 'You think she's in danger?'

'Not from others. From herself.'

Sometimes he gets a little confusing, Williams thought peevishly. He waited patiently for Sivo to explain.

The inspector sighed and turned to face the sergeant. 'We can't rule her out as a suspect. If it were anyone else, I'd ask for a warrant.' He pointed a finger and said firmly. 'And I'm not hesitant because she's my friend's daughter. If she did it, it wasn't premeditated.' He shook his head. 'But why the hell did she run?'

'What did you find out from Riley?'

'He said he had sent her to somewhere to interview someone about one of his ongoing investigations. That's all he would say.' His face was grim. 'But I'm not finished with that bastard yet.'

'What was involved?'

Sivo shrugged. 'A tourist made a serious complaint to his office.'

'Does it concern this case?'

'Of course it does. Otherwise he would have been more forthcoming,' Sivo said irritably. 'Damn silly question.' He swung his chair to face the window. 'And the Garland woman will tell me about the girl's quarrel with her mother, or I'll know the reason why.' He paused. 'Carter says Juliet accused her daughter of spying on her. I'm sure he believes that, but it doesn't make sense. Amy didn't need to spy, and Juliet Carter knew that. She has never hidden her light under a bushel.'

CHAPTER EIGHT

They left Olaf and the boat at two o'clock, and with the picnic hamper on the back seat of their hired car, drove to the nearest hotel. Mack left Emma to order tea while he looked for a telephone. He called the number Carter had given them. Carter answered.

Mack said: 'You still there? We're coming over.'

Carter's tone reflected his eagerness. 'Have you found her?'

'Sorry, no. But we have something. We don't know how important, but we'll talk when we get there.'

'Where are you now?'

'At the Pearl Palace Hotel.'

'Only ten minutes from the theatre.'

'Give me half an hour. While we're on our way over, see if Uva Point can tell you about boats leaving the island between eight and ten this morning.'

'Any reason?'

'Someone got to Crab Island just before we did.'

'Trouble?' Carter sounded anxious.

'He must have heard us coming. We heard his engine start up on the other side of the island; the eastern shore.'

'I'll have the information before you arrive.'

'Is anyone with you?'

'No. I'm alone.'

'See you in half an hour.'

By the time Mack returned to the crowded hotel restaurant, the waiter had served the tea. His daughter-in-law had found a table near the window. Tourists of every shape, dressed in clothes of every hue filled every corner of the huge restaurant space. Mack concluded that everyone was speaking at once. He grimaced. 'Noisy.'

Emma nodded, sipped her tea and put the cup down. 'At least we won't be overheard.'

Mack kicked the hamper at her feet. 'Do you want to look through the photos again?'

Emma gave a decisive shake of her head. 'I saw enough on our way from Crab Island. Just as well you insisted we look at them before anyone else sees them.'

'I've had enough experience with dodgy photos to know this is a sensitive situation. We don't know the extent of Carter's involvement.' He looked pensive. 'Or if he isn't involved, how much he will be hurt by the disclosures.' He looked disturbed. 'These should really be burnt.'

Emma's alarm was instant. 'You wouldn't?'

'Why not? They're not evidence.'

'I feel in my bones that somewhere in those prints is enough evidence to hang a murderer.'

'They don't hang people in Pascua.'

'Well whatever they do to them.'

He sighed. 'You're right, of course. Which ones do you want to show Carter?'

Emma knew Mack had already decided what he was going to do, but his question was a measure of his respect for her, and she was grateful.

'We've sorted them into three piles. Dicey, dodgy and definitely not. Let's hold back the definitely—the nudes—until we know whether Carter is involved. The other two piles have faces I want identified. Two photos in particular interest me. Carter may know the subjects.'

Mack was silent for a moment. 'You suggest we hold back all the pictures except two?'

Emma nodded. 'No need to produce the others yet.' She looked thoughtful. 'I know I'm only a simple country girl, but I can never understand how people can derive pleasure from that.' She kicked the box at her feet.

'Well, as Jane Austen said, *one half of the world cannot understand the pleasures of the other.*'

She looked at him askance. 'What is this fascination with Jane Austen?'

He held up his right hand. 'I swear we're only good friends.'

Emma laughed out loud. 'Idiot.'

He smiled. 'Agreed then.' He grew serious. 'The two you want to show Carter: they are the ones you looked at so intently, and then so thoughtfully.' It wasn't a question. Mack shook his head slowly. 'I wish I'd had you on my team when I was in the business.'

'Why, thank you kind sir. How discerning you are.'

'Those caught my interest too. If Carter can't identify them, we have to look elsewhere.'

'I know what you're thinking, but it will need a great deal of legwork.'

Mack sat back and laughed. 'You've even got the jargon. Now we'll *have* to go into business.'

She smiled. 'It would be fun.'

He frowned. 'Fun isn't a word I'd use. It's a dangerous business; there's a killer out there. Remember, a killer won't hesitate to kill again to cover the evidence of the first murder. He has nothing to lose.'

Emma shuddered. 'You're making me nervous.'

'Good. Stay nervous. It's safer.' He paused for a long moment. 'I wasn't sure whether to tell you this but . . .'

'About the car that followed us down the mountain road this morning.' She nodded. 'I saw your intense interest in the rear-view mirror.'

'And I concluded that if someone was following us, this is bigger than I thought. I wondered if we should be meddling in it.'

She looked at him inquiringly. 'But you've decided we had to go on? For Amy?' She waited for him to speak. 'You did, right?'

'We may be getting in over our heads. We should stop and leave it to Sivo.'

She shook her head stubbornly. 'We're in this now and I'm certainly not giving up; especially while Amy is still missing.'

'I'm not suggesting we give up looking for Amy, but I want you to promise me you'll follow my instructions every foot of the way.'

Solemnly she held up her hand. 'I promise.' She smiled. 'I'm glad they made you come, Daddy Dear.'

Mack snorted. 'Any more of that Daddy Dear, and I'll pack you off home at once.' He looked at her disapprovingly. 'Teig insisted because he loves you. We all love you, and if you end up in trouble, Grampa will skin me alive.' Mack was gratified to see that she was suitably repentant. He stood up. 'Let's go. Carter's waiting.'

When they went out into the brilliant sunshine, they could see bathers rolling and tumbling in the foaming waves while on the horizon sails drooped and yachts barely moved on the calm, cobalt sea.

*   *   *

Blaine Carter turned the pictures towards him. Mack and Emma sat quite still as he looked carefully at each face in turn. The empty theatre was quiet with a stillness that seemed to reflect their tensions as they waited for him to speak. The office smelt of old books and furniture polish. She looked at the bookshelves, the panelled walls and the dreary curtains. She looked at Carter and shifted slightly, quietly, careful not to break his

107

concentration. I wonder if there is a separate kind of smell for dead careers, she thought moodily. If there was, this place would reek of it; or why would anyone want to bring a successful career to this end of the world where there was little hope to emerge from the pack. Guiltily she shook off her morbid thoughts. Amy's father was a decent man enmeshed in an indecent situation of which he was completely oblivious.

Carter looked up and sighed. 'Juliet, Ray Dickens and Harry Naish who worked for me until six months ago. This one is Senator Morrison from New Jersey, and this is Mrs Reinholt from Perth. They both came to one of Juliet's evenings. They are the only faces I recognize. The others are strangers. They may have come to the theatre—Juliet brought a lot of people here—but I don't remember them.'

Emma hid her disappointment. 'And the other photo?'

'Don't you want to know who passed Uva Point before you?'

Mack nodded. 'That first, I think.'

'Fifteen boats of the type you described passed the point before you did this morning. Thirteen were charters with at least six on board. We can discard them. Of the other two, one was a private boat owned by Howard Bruneau which went out at a quarter past seven.' He was silent as he looked at his pad. 'Two people were on board complete with fishing gear. The other one had a single occupant who gave the name Rogers and a bed-and-breakfast address. The B-and-B don't have a Rogers staying there. It was hired from Bay Charter. I spoke to Benny Crowe who was on duty at the yard this morning. He says the person who took the boat out was dressed in oilskin trousers, a leather jacket buttoned to the neck and a balaclava, dark glasses with a muffler around the neck and covering the mouth. Under the circumstances he would have been lucky to identify Santa Claus. He didn't care as long as the book was signed and the fee paid. That was probably your intruder.'

'Who is Bruneau?'

'A member of a highly respected Island family. They live in a quaint home, the Château La Brède up at Bougainville on the coast road to Largo Point.'

Mack smiled. 'Having appropriated the name, I hope the château is a copy of the original in France.'

Carter looked at him with surprise. 'Bravo. You know it then?'

'I passed through Gironde during the war. I saw the château and read up on it.' He gestured apologetically. 'I have an insatiable curiosity about things I see and don't know about.'

Emma laughed. 'Just don't tell him your middle name. He'll know all about you in a twinkling.'

'The Bruneau family built a miniature of the original. Amy was fascinated by it. She was a close friend of the youngest Bruneau girl. She often stayed there.'

Mack pointed to the photograph. 'This won't get the baby bathed. What about this?'

Carter looked at Emma as he turned the print towards him. 'You found these on Crab Island? In my house?'

Emma nodded. 'Yes. In the bathroom. On the floor.' She picked out two prints. 'These were on the path. It's likely the intruder dropped them.'

'I see.' He looked at the photos for a moment and then looked at her. There was a long silence.

'Well?'

She shrugged. 'That's it. I found them in the bathroom.'

Carter rose from his desk and walked to the bookcase. He fingered the spines of the bound scripts as though seeking something familiar to which he could cling. Stress was evident in the set of his mouth.

Mack said: 'You see we . . .'

'Wait!' Carter spoke without turning. 'Don't say anything that will entangle you in a web of sophistry.' He paused. 'When I read a script for the first time, I read the last act first. From that I can determine the quality of the play. It saves me a hell of a lot of wasted time reading dozens of plays. It may sound weird to you, but

110

it's one of my idiosyncrasies and it works for me.' He walked to the window and turned to face them. 'I've been waiting for your final act, but there isn't one.' He sat at his desk. 'You told me on the phone that you had something; and then you show me two innocuous photographs and ask me to identify the subjects. And I ask myself why.' He looked at each of them in turn. 'I'm not an idiot, so don't treat me like one. As a director of nearly a hundred plays, I know more about human follies and foibles than you will learn in your lifetime.' He paused and jabbed a finger at the photograph. 'This doesn't mean a thing to me, but clearly it has some significance for you.' He looked at them angrily. 'Now, who's going to tell me what this is about?'

His guests exchanged embarrassed glances. Emma said quickly: 'It's my fault, Mr Carter. I wasn't sure what you knew about the parties at Crab Island. I wanted to tread water until we knew what you knew. We had no intention of deceiving you.'

Mack said quietly: 'It was a decision we had both agreed upon. It was a matter of respect for your sensibilities.' He stood up and walked to the window. 'We felt that while you were concerned and overwrought about the murder and Amy's disappearance, you didn't need any disturbing revelations.'

Carter said resignedly: 'I knew enough about the parties at Crab Island to know I wanted no part of them.'

Mack nodded. 'It was a question of degree. We realized you weren't completely ignorant of what was going on, but as outsiders we . . .'

'You didn't want to get involved. Is that it?'

'No, you're wrong,' Emma said firmly. 'We're already involved, but as outsiders we had no right to—how can I put this without being offensive—prejudge your perception or degree of complaisance.'

Carter said sardonically: 'You wondered how far I had dug my head into the sand?'

Emma felt a growing exasperation. 'I realize our sensitivity was probably misplaced but . . .'

'I prefer the whole truth.'

Mack went back to his chair. He said firmly: 'If that's what you want, you'll have it.' Emma's exasperation was like a contagion. He was sick of all this; sick of people whose images were frozen on a batch of photographs he would have preferred to consign to the nearest fire. Carter was a decent man, but he had lived his life exactly as he had so sarcastically described it; with his head in the sand. Mack pushed one of the photos across the table. 'But first, do you know who that is?'

Carter looked down at the group. 'I told you. I know only the three people I named.'

Mack pushed the other photo across to him. He placed his finger on the face of a girl smiling up at the camera. The image had a large circle drawn around her head.

'Do you know who this is?'

Carter looked perplexed. 'You know damn well who it is. You—' He stopped. 'Oh damn. I forgot. You've never seen her. You've never seen any of them, have you?'

Mack turned to Emma. 'Emma dear, please go down to the car and bring me all the photos. All of them. The dicey, the dodgy and the definitely not.'

'Wait.' Carter gave Emma an agonized look. There was a long pause. It was clear he was finding it difficult to speak. 'Are there any compromising pictures of Juliet in that lot?'

Mack shook his head. He put his finger on one of the photos on the table. 'That's the only photo of Juliet in the whole pile.'

Carter sighed with relief. 'Then bring the rest up.'

CHAPTER NINE

The director of the Pascua Tourist Board was, as befitted the head of a department that dealt with public matters, ensconced in the most luxurious suite on the top floor of the Justice Building overlooking Pascua Bay and Uva Point. From his desk, he could look up from his papers to see the boats in the channel. His favourite occupation, though, was not his work but watching the cruise liners leaving the bay, accompanied by fussing tugs, and with decks lined with the rich and famous.

James Riley, the director, occupied a corner office that looked both west and south. Riley was a man who believed that he had an undeniable right to the best things in life. He dressed well in a fashion which, while it might not perhaps be universally acceptable amongst the *haut monde* of the world's capitals, was admired by socialites on the islands, and not a few of the tourists from the mainland who called at his office.

When Sivo arrived on the tenth floor he found Riley in high spirits, having just been invited to the Prime Minister's mansion for dinner, an item of news which he threw off casually as a matter of little importance but which, the inspector knew, was an event which would be mentioned just as casually to all his socialite friends for the next week.

Reacting to the sight of Riley in a handsome grey suit with cuffs and cuff links visible, and a tie that could have been taken for any public-school tie, but which in fact was not, Sivo said: 'I like the suit. Rehearsing for the great day?'

Riley smiled. 'You know damn well the event is black tie.' He motioned to a chair. Sivo smiled inwardly as Riley touched the wave in his hair.

'I thought Carter was going to be busy at the theatre all morning?'

'He was.'

'Then who took his boat out?'

Sivo frowned. 'Went out this morning, did it? Are you sure?'

'I'd know the *Amyrillis* if it was pitch dark. I've been over to Crab often enough in her. Anyway, what brings you up here?'

Sivo leaned back in the big comfortable chair feigning complete lack of interest in the *Amyrillis*.

'I'm back on the same track as I was this morning. I want to know where you sent Amy Carter.'

Riley shook his head. 'And I have to give you the same answer. That's classified.'

'For God's sake, Riley. We're living on an island the size of a piss-pot in a republic half the world doesn't know exists.' Sivo was angry and he wanted Riley to know it. 'We haven't got a damned secret service, so don't act as if you are one.'

Riley flushed at the contempt in the man's voice. 'I'm sure the Prime Minister will be interested in your elegant description of his manor.'

'You'll have an opportunity to tell him next week. It can be the subject of some sparkling dinner conversation.' Sivo stood up angrily and walked to the window. 'As he has given me *carte blanche* on this case, I think he will be more interested in the fact that you are hampering a murder investigation.' He turned and looked at Riley with venom. 'One in which a prominent member of his circle is a victim.' Sivo placed both hands on the desk and leaned towards Riley. 'Now are you going to give me that information or must I communicate with the Prime Minister's office?'

Riley thought for a moment. He knew the extent of Sivo's considerable influence and was afraid of it, but to give him what he wanted was inconceivable. He decided on subterfuge. 'A tourist from Sydney approached us with a complaint about a conman operating on the island. She lost a considerable sum of money. We have a suspect and I sent Amy Carter with a photograph to Sydney to interview the tourist.' He shuffled papers on his desk. 'After that she was to continue on to London to join the marketing division of our tourist office there.'

Sivo straightened up and looked hard at Riley. 'Who else on your staff knew of this?'

'No one else,' Riley said sullenly. His ego was badly dented, but his pleasure at believing he had bested the policeman was mixed with apprehension. Sivo was a dangerous enemy. If he discovered Riley's equivocation, there was no future for him in Pascua.

'What's this tourist's name?' Sivo took a notebook and pen from his pocket. 'And the address?'

Riley nearly collapsed with shock, but fear gave him courage. He was like a trapped animal that goes straight for his tormentor.

'I can't tell you that. This is my fief. We have always protected the identity of tourists who come to us. I've given you enough to satisfy the Prime Minister if he is called into this.' He looked at Sivo defiantly. 'Have you found her car yet?'

'No, but we will. When was Amy Carter due back?'

'It was at her discretion. When she had completed her assignment in London.' He shrugged. 'A few weeks; a couple of months.'

Sivo stared at him. Then he nodded.

'Yeah, right.'

He realized it wasn't exactly a sparkling exit line, but the American inflection gave him a great deal of satisfaction. He went out of the door, shutting it gently behind him.

Riley pressed a button on his intercom. His secretary answered at once.

'Yes, Mr Riley.'

'Have you heard from Miss Carter yet?'

'No, Mr Riley. Grant telephoned to say her car is definitely not in any of the car parks in the city.'

'Get him on the phone at once.'

'I'll try his office.'

Riley waited impatiently, pacing around the office and staring occasionally at the view from his window. When the phone rang he snatched at it.

'Riley.'

'It's Grant, Mr Riley.'

'Where the hell have you been? Why didn't you call when you got back from Crab Island?'

'There was nothing to report. I searched from seven until I saw a boat coming towards the island. I told your skipper to make a run for it. I'm positive she's not there.'

'Did you search the house?'

'Every inch.'

'Did you look in the attic?'

'What attic? I didn't know there was one.'

Riley thought for a moment. He realized it was a stupid question. He was the only outsider who knew of the attic. He replaced the receiver without a word. 'Damn! Damn the girl,' he said viciously. He reached for a bottle in the bottom drawer of his desk, his hand trembling with a mixture of anger and apprehension.

Downstairs, Sivo opened the door of his office on the fourth floor. Williams looked up from his reports.

'What did you find out?'

'Nothing new. Only what I've known for years.'

Williams looked puzzled. 'What's that?'

'Riley is a damned poor liar.' He sat at his desk. 'Someone took Carter's boat out today.'

Williams looked surprised and then thoughtful.

'Amy Carter's two chums? Do you think they went to Crab Island?'

Sivo nodded. 'Of course. But you know the

118

rule.'

Williams smiled. 'I know the rule. Check everything. Right?'

'Right. I'm going down to the theatre to see Carter.' He put his notebook on his desk. 'Has forensics come up with a cast of that tyre-track yet?'

'They'll send it over in half an hour.'

'You sent a soil sample from the immediate vicinity?'

'Exactly as you instructed. Ten small bags of dirt from all around the tyre-track.'

Sivo frowned. 'That session at the theatre was a dead waste of time.'

Williams looked surprised.

'I wondered why you got them all together. It isn't good . . .' He stopped, embarrassed.

'Go on, say it. It isn't acceptable procedure.' He nodded. 'Agreed, but sometimes when a lot of people get talking, someone is spooked by something that's said. Then they do something foolish.'

Williams looked puzzled. 'So sometimes it can be acceptable.'

'Sometimes it's worked for me.' He looked fiercely at Williams. 'But don't you try it until you're qualified to do it.' He made for the door. 'Or until you're a genius like me.'

He went out, leaving Williams shaking his head.

'Sometimes he can be so damned childish,' he said.

*　　*　　*

Emma leaned over to the picnic-box on the back seat of the car. She began to drag it towards her, then she looked up, to see Sivo swinging in to the kerb behind her. She left the box on the seat and closed the car door.

Sivo walked towards her. He was smiling. Her heart sank. What did Grampa say? *When enemies smile, be ready.* He wasn't exactly an enemy, but close enough.

'Hello, Inspector. Nice to see you again.'

The big man smiled, but only with his mouth. 'I'm happy to see you too, Mrs Olsen.' His smile disappeared. 'Have a nice outing today, then?'

Her heart plummeted. Be ready. 'It was lovely, Inspector.'

'Good. Let's go inside, shall we? We can talk more about it in Blaine's office. McGlashan up there, is he?' She nodded dumbly. 'Good. Well, bring along whatever it was you came down to fetch.'

'I came to get the car keys. I realized I'd left them in the ignition.' She held up the keys for his inspection.

'Right.' He took her arm and led her to the theatre door.

When they walked into the office, Carter looked up in surprise. His first instinct was to move the photographs to a desk drawer, but anything he did now would draw attention to them. Mack showed no sign that he was perturbed by the inspector's presence. Greetings over, Blaine waited for the inspector to come to the point of his visit. Sivo held a chair for Emma and then sat on the sofa. There was a long silence. Sivo looked at each of them in turn. Mack, Emma and Blaine were nonplussed as the silence dragged on. Then Sivo feigned sudden enlightenment.

'Oh dear. Have I interrupted something important?'

'Not at all,' Carter waved a dismissive hand. 'We were talking about Crab Island.'

'Indeed. Wonderful property.' He looked at Mack. 'Did you enjoy the excursion?'

'To the island?' Mack was caught unawares.

Sivo smiled. 'Of course. That was where you went today, wasn't it?'

'Oh. Oh yes. To Crab Island.' Mack thought for a moment. 'It was interesting.'

Emma nodded. 'Yes, interesting. Interesting and enjoyable. We had a fine day for it.'

Sivo went to the window as though to check her assertion on the merits of the day.

'Interesting?' He was incredulous. 'Interesting? Is that all you can say about the habitat of the world's largest crab?' He smiled disarmingly at Carter. 'I would ban them from Crab for ever.' He looked at Mack. 'You weren't there long. Something bring you back in a hurry?' He walked to the desk, and without seeming to pounce, picked up the two photographs. 'I see these were taken at Crab.' He looked at Carter and smiled. 'In front of that saucy picture of yours, Blaine. Were these taken today?'

He shook his head. 'Silly of me. Of course not. You couldn't have processed them so soon.'

He looked at the photo for a moment. He said softly, as though to himself, 'Besides, Mrs Phillips wasn't with you today.' He threw the photos down as though they were of no further interest to him.

Mack looked quizzically at the inspector. 'You know Mrs Phillips?'

Sivo looked at him with astonishment. 'Know her? Of course I know her. We have her in protective custody at her hotel.'

Carter was appalled. 'Protective custody? Sylvia Phillips? Harry Martin's daughter? Why? Has she seen a lawyer?'

'Dear me, yes. It was the first thing she asked for. It's the first thing they all ask for. Everybody watches American films these days.'

'Why protective custody? Is she in danger?'

Sivo smiled. 'Only from herself.' He picked up the photo, looked at it and replaced it. 'She persisted in denying she had ever been to Crab Island.' He went back to the sofa. 'But she admitted it eventually.' He looked at Emma. 'So these came back with you from the island?'

Mack realized at once that the inspector was toying with them. A lesser man would have thought that he was merely tormenting them, but Mack, a skilled investigator himself, recognized the slow, devious and dangerous technique of an experienced inquisitor. But the technique was a two-edged sword. To one who listened carefully without agitation or panic, the extent of the interrogator's information is revealed. Sivo had already given him several facts, the most significant of which was that Crab Island had assumed some importance to his investigation. The fact that Sylvia Phillips was now obviously crucial to Sivo's inquiries was a major surprise to Mack. However, had he known before the inspector announced it that the encircled head in the photo belonged to Harry Martin's daughter, he would have given more weight to her role in the affair.

Mack looked at Emma as she answered the inspector. 'I found them on the floor of one of the bedrooms. We were admiring the house.'

The inspector said drily: 'There's a lot to admire. Were these the only ones you brought back?'

Here's the tricky one, Mack thought. We dare not lie about this. He said quickly: 'There were some others, Inspector, but they are Mr Carter's property.'

Carter shook his head. 'I'm sorry, Joe. I haven't had an opportunity to look through them yet. I'll be sure to let you have any that may help in your investigation.' He smiled. 'But I hardly think we'll find anything useful amongst some picnic photos.'

Sivo walked to the door. 'Not amongst picnic photos. No.'

Mack caught the irony in his tone and looked at Emma. Her glance told him she was alert to Sivo's disenchantment with the limits Carter had placed on how much he was prepared to divulge.

Mack looked at Carter. His unspoken question was correctly interpreted by Carter, who nodded. Mack said: 'We had an unexpected visitor at the island, Inspector.'

'Of course you did. Someone in dark glasses and balaclava.' There was a long silence. 'Uva Point office reported that to my office.' He continued in a tone of heavy irony. 'I'm sure you'll keep me posted if you come across anything else that's relevant. Please don't believe I know everything.'

As the inspector opened the door, Carter said: 'Have you any leads in your search for Amy?'

Sivo paused. 'I'm sorry, Blaine. I've nothing to tell you.'

'And Juliet? When can we bring her home? I have to make arrangements fo . . .' He stopped, stood up quickly and walked to the window.

Sivo said quietly: 'I'll let you know soon.'

As he moved to the door, Mack said: 'Oh, Inspector.' Sivo stopped. 'Are your men following us?'

'You are being followed? Did you see who was following you?'

'I saw the car, and I'm convinced we were being watched on our way from the jetty to the hotel where we had tea.'

Sivo shook his head. 'No, there is no reason for anyone on my staff to follow you.' He looked thoughtful as he turned to the door. 'Get in touch with me immediately if you have a licence number.'

'I'll do that, Inspector.'

Sivo went out, shutting the door softly behind him.

Carter turned. Emma saw his eyes glistening. She stood up. 'Would you like us to move to a hotel?'

'No. No of course not.' He was controlling himself with an effort. 'I'm not coming back here tonight. I've made arrangements for Culum Garrett to hold the fort.' He went back to his desk.

Mack nodded, stood up and went to the door. 'I can think of no better place to talk than in the quiet of your home. I'll go down and bring up the remaining photographs. You can study them before we talk at home.' He went out, returning a short while later with the picnic box.

There was a soft knock at the door. Blaine

called out and the door opened. Rhoda Larkin walked in.

'Oh. I'm sorry, Blaine. Shall I come back later?'

'It isn't necessary. My guests are just leaving.'

After brief introductions, Mack and Emma took their leave.

*　　　*　　　*

The inspector bounced into his office humming the opening number from *Oklahoma!* Williams smiled.

'And why is it a beautiful morning? And it isn't still morning.'

'Not only the morning but the whole day.' He went to the window and sniffed. It was almost as though he could taste the salt air through the closed double glazing. 'Look at that sea. There's nothing more lovely than a view of the ocean.'

Williams rubbed his tousled hair with inky fingers. 'Especially if you've solved a murder. Have you?'

Sivo kept his eyes on the view. 'What? Solved the murder?' He turned and winked at his subordinate. 'Not quite, but we're getting there. Fast.'

'Has Carter confessed? I know. Juliet Carter committed suicide.'

'If you're going to be facetious, I'll see you

126

spend the next few months in Records.' He sat at his desk. 'Right. Now listen and take notes. I might forget something.'

'Right, and the Prime Minister is my dad.' His wry tribute to Sivo's extraordinary memory left the inspector unmoved. Williams stood up, went to the stationery cupboard for another pad.

Sivo looked at him speculatively. Although the lad was half his age, there was a bond between them which had grown out of their reliance on the other's integrity. Furthermore they were able to communicate on the same level of good humour without transcending the bounds of acceptable behaviour. Their respect for one another's abilities was an important ingredient of their association. Williams was still unmarried and lived with an elder married sister. Sivo knew he was walking out with one of the civilian clerks in the Justice Department. She was a girl for whom Sivo had often expressed approval and he had often remarked, too, that Williams needed a good woman to settle him down.

As Williams walked back to his desk, the inspector shook off his reverie. He looked at his notes.

'Fact. Two months ago we had a sniff of some kind of criminal activity involving tourists. Because it was only a vague whisper, we passed it on to Riley's department for investigation and confirmation. We expected him to pass it back if there was a hint of anything illegal.' He looked at Williams. 'Got that?'

Williams finished a sentence and looked up. 'Got it. And now you think there was something?'

'There you go again.' The inspector was exasperated. 'How often must I repeat myself? Develop an orderly mind. Go from fact to fact. Don't jump around like an animated jackrabbit.'

Williams looked back at his notes. 'Sorry, Inspector.'

'You'll be sorrier if I have to tell you again.' Sivo scratched his nose and swivelled to face the window.

'Fact. Carter said Juliet told him she was in trouble and needed his help, but she is killed before he gets home.' He thought for a moment. 'Fact. During interrogation at the theatre, everyone was rushing in to alibi everyone else.'

'But we accepted—for the time being at least—that their alibis were sound.'

'Not entirely. Remember, it was Haig or A.N. Other in that chair. I wouldn't trust a single one of that lot. Every one of them told at least one lie.'

Williams looked at him thoughtfully. 'You don't trust anyone, do you?'

Sivo swivelled back to face him. 'I trust my wife and anyone I've known for sixty years.'

'But you're only fifty-two.'

'You've got it in one. Let's go on. Fact. Carter had a photograph on his desk with the members of the Carter Company holding up glasses and toasting Sylvia as if she was the Queen of the May.' He looked up at the ceiling. 'I ask myself why a girl who is almost a stranger is given the full treatment.' He looked down at Williams. 'And why that same girl lies about going to a party at Crab Island.'

Williams looked up to see Sivo regarding him expectantly. Light dawned. 'Something happened there that she would rather keep to herself.'

Sivo beamed. 'Well put.'

'Where is the photo now?'

'Carter has it.'

'Why didn't you take it?'

'Because I didn't want him to know how important it is until I get a warrant.'

'Then he doesn't know that it's important?'

'No. I'm convinced he isn't involved in anything that occurred out there.' He paused. 'What do you know about Victor Bellamy?'

'He's a photographer.'

'I know he's a ruddy photographer. He has that seedy little shop in Parrot Lane. I asked you if you know anything about him.'

Williams frowned. 'All I know is that he is one of fifty licensed photographers in Pascua. He takes clear pictures, and that's all that can be said for them. He's not very good, and a lot

129

of his trade is a bit sleazy. Why do you ask?'

'His name was stamped in tiny letters on the back of those photos. Just his name. No logo or trade name.' He looked at his notes. 'Did you ask Uva Point about Carter's boat?'

'They listed Olaf's passengers as Mrs Olsen and Mr Mack.'

Sivo nodded. 'Close enough.'

Williams frowned. 'They also said Carter was inquiring about someone who left before Olaf went out. They said it was a hire with one occupant. That boat arrived back at eleven-fifteen.'

Sivo's smile was beatific. 'Fact. Carter is interested in someone who goes past Uva before his guests leave the Bay.'

Williams frowned. 'Why is that important?'

'How would he know about the second boat? Because Olsen and McGlashan told him. And how would they know about a boat that left the Bay before they even got to Crab Island?'

Williams smiled an enlightened smile. 'Because they saw the occupant at the island.'

'Bingo.'

Williams shook his head. 'I don't know. Aren't you reaching a bit for that one?'

'Of course. We're always reaching until the facts are proven. Our job is to get the proof.' He stood up. 'It's called police work.' He stretched and looked across the bay. 'And isn't it a fascinating pastime?'

Williams said gloomily: 'Fascinating.'

'Now comes the difficult part.'

'Proving it.' Williams sighed. 'Lots of legwork.' He watched the inspector scribbling in his notebook. 'My guess is we begin at Crab Island.'

Sivo ticked his notes. 'Crab Island, Mrs Garland, another spell with Sylvia Phillips and a trip to the country.'

'The country? Where in the country?'

'To visit the Château La Brède.'

'La Brède? Why go there?'

The inspector was enjoying himself. He smiled broadly. 'Didn't someone mention Howard Bruneau?'

'Yes, but he was just mentioned in passing. He went out fishing.'

'I love things that are mentioned just in passing. They often lead to some things of importance.' He went to the door.

Williams followed him, shaking his head. A complete waste of time, he thought irritably. It would be a cold day in hell if they proved Howard Bruneau had anything to do with the death of Juliet Carter.

CHAPTER TEN

Rhoda Larkin sat in front of Blaine's desk, opened her black file cover and drew out her designs for *Look for Me Tomorrow*, the play scheduled for the new year. She passed them across the desk and was shocked at the change in him since she had spoken to him in the greenroom. He was pale and his eyes were red, almost as though he had been weeping.

In a neutral tone she said: 'Would you like to leave this until tomorrow?'

Blaine stood up and walked to the window. 'No, I'll be all right in a moment.' He looked down into the street where Emma and Mack were just getting into her car. He watched as they drove away. 'That's a remarkable girl.'

'Who is she?'

'Amy's friend. They were at school together.' He rubbed his forehead. 'Will you excuse me for a moment. I'd like to freshen up. Splash some water on my face.'

'Of course.' All at once as he turned to go, Rhoda sensed that there was more to his unhappiness than the death of his wife and the disappearance of his daughter. He appeared to be surrounded by an aura of defeat; filled with that quality which is evident when there is no longer any spirit of resistance against adversity. His shoulders were slumped and his eyes reminded her of a beaten animal.

She wished she had his talent for words. He was a compassionate man, and at times when his encouragement was needed he was always there with the appropriate expressions of comfort. It was sad that there was no one to do the same for him. While she herself was kind and compassionate, she was unwilling to assume that role. Rhoda Larkin was not emotionally equipped to take on that responsibility.

She had always been a private person, the only child of an adventurous couple whose aim in life appeared to be an ambition to sail their fifty-foot yacht to every glamorous destination on the planet. However their ambitious plans did not include the burden of an introverted and shy little girl. She was shipped off to a boarding-school, the Convent of Our Lady of Fatima, located on the island of Pascua Petit. She recalled the number of times their ambition brought them to Pascua, when they would take her to lunch, after which her mother would say: 'Must run, darling. Have to catch the tide. See you in the spring. I'll write, I promise.' And with Sister Madeline holding her hand, the sad, lonely little girl would watch from Uva Point as the yacht, with full sails, disappeared over the horizon.

Yes, she could recall exactly how many times they had visited Pascua in the ten years she had been at the convent. It was eleven, one less than the number of precious letters she had received and hoarded in her photograph album.

When they had perished in a storm off Tierra del Fuego, her father's brother flew out from London to break the news and let her know she could stay at the convent or continue her schooling in England. She chose to go to London where she studied as an industrial designer, but switched to theatrical design when she realized she had no future in industry. When her residence permit expired, she returned to the land of her birth at a time when the Carter Company was looking for a replacement for a series of unsuitable phoneys. She got the job and it became all she ever wanted to do.

With her inheritance she bought a large building site on South Shore Drive, and designed the house of her dreams where she had lived for over a decade. Her only companions were a fox-terrier, a parrot and a Polynesian live-in couple who bullied and adored her. But her loneliness was an ever-present reminder of her school years.

She was happy at the Carter Theatre. Every opening night when she viewed the play from the VIP box as Carter's guest and the curtain went up on her designs, she felt the pleasure of fulfilment which never diminished with time. Each new play brought with it the exquisite anticipation of that moment of silence between the overture and the rise of the curtain.

It was a long time before she admitted to herself that the pleasure she felt was in sharing that moment with the man with whom she had fallen in love. That moment came on a night the audience gave the cast a standing ovation at the final curtain and in a spirit of exuberance, Carter hugged her, laughed delightedly and kissed her on the forehead. She knew his reaction was merely relief that every facet of a fairly difficult play had coalesced into a production of which they could be proud.

But for her it was an unwelcome revelation.

She never shared his box again. At first he was puzzled and hurt, but he finally accepted her excuse that opening nights were too stressful. She said she preferred to see the play once the reviews were in. Last night in the office when he took her hand, she had been overcome with love and pity, and had made her escape as soon as she could. In bed, until the early hours, she wrestled with the problem of her future with the company and whether she should move on. When she heard of the murder this morning, she knew her decision would have to be delayed for a month at least.

She heard his footsteps in the passage, and she went quickly to the bookcase to compose herself. When he came through the open door, she had her back to him as she turned the pages of *The Cat and the Canary.*

He went to the desk. She hesitated for a moment before replacing the book.

'Interesting play.'

'Which one were you looking at?'

'*The Cat and The Canary.*'

He nodded his agreement. 'It can be wonderful entertainment if played in the right style.' He sat back, at ease in familiar territory. 'It's often presented as a comedy. I suppose it's the film version starring Bob Hope that began the trend. That style is a mistake on stage. The later—the Edward Fox film version—is the definitive one. It has to be played as a serious mystery with loads of business to keep the audience on the edge of their seats. Done like that it's a great vehicle for horror. It has two wonderfully terrifying curtains at the ends of the first and second acts.' He spread his hands. 'You've got the writer's intention right there.'

As he talked, she could only think of the way his expression relaxed and his eyes came alive. She said: 'It might be a good idea to revive it.'

He smiled. 'It was one of my first efforts. It was great fun. Lots of scope for some exciting business.' He grew serious. 'I'm not sure that it will fit into our programme.'

She laughed. 'If you do it I promise to stay on for a while.' She could have bitten her tongue. She had rehearsed her resignation speech so many times that it had stayed at the forefront of her mind until it escaped unbidden.

His expression froze. 'You're leaving? Why? When?' He was stunned. Suddenly the animation and ebullience disappeared. 'I didn't know. Did Wendy forget to give me your letter?'

She was flustered and confused. Words wouldn't come.

He looked away. 'I understand. Things have gotten out of hand. I'm not even sure I am capable of directing a good play any more.' He shrugged. 'I had thought once or twice about accepting a good offer from a hotel chain.'

'Oh no.' She was appalled. 'You can't close the theatre. It means so much to so many people. It's a wonderful asset to Pascua.' She took his hand across the desk. 'You're a fine director. Your work still has significance.'

He leaned back, his expression a mask of misery and defeat. He stood up and went to the bookcase. He stood for a long time with his back to her. Finally he turned and when he spoke his voice was underscored with anguish.

'Damn it, Rhoda. I can't do it without you.' He flung out his arms as he went back to the desk. 'There you have it.' He spoke vehemently. 'I can't do it without you.'

She shook her head miserably. 'Yes you can. Anyway, this is a bad time to be considering these decisions.'

'This has nothing to do with the present

circumstances.' His voice rose. 'It goes way back. Do you understand what I'm saying? Every time you came into the office the whole day brightened. Every time I saw you I forgot the dreadful misery of my life; my marriage. I . . .'

'No, Blaine. Please stop. I can't listen to this.' Her mind cried out: No! This isn't the way I wanted it. This isn't the time. She banged her fist on the table. All my life, she thought, I believed that one day, under a blue sky or over a candle-lit dinner, someone would say *I love you. Marry me.* Not now. Not like this. All at once she realized that the illogical rejection of his words was conditioned by the ersatz romantic world of make-believe in which she had been immersed for so long. She said softly, 'I can't listen to this.'

'You have to listen. Then you can walk out of that door and make up your mind whether to come back or not. But you will listen.' He stood up and went to the window. 'For obvious reasons. I couldn't say these things before. Now perhaps when I *can* say them, the moment is inappropriate, but if I don't speak now I . . .'

'No, Blaine. It *is* inappropriate.'

He shrugged. 'Then so be it. I love you Rhoda. I've loved you for years.' He turned and looked out of the window. 'There, I've said it. If I have offended you, I can only say I'm glad I told you how I feel.'

She stood up and walked to the door. 'I'll stay on a while. Blaine. It is a decision I can't make lightly.' She turned at the door and looked at him. 'I'm not offended, Blaine. If circumstances were different, I would even have been overjoyed. But for now I can only ask for time to consider my options.' She went to the door.

He said bitterly: 'You didn't tell me why you're going. Or even where.' She did not look back but just shook her head and with tears flowing, went out.

Carter stood for a long time staring at the door, willing her to come back and speak to him. Finally he walked to the window and stared down at the street. He saw her blue Ford on the other side of the street. She did not look up, but he knew she was aware of him looking down at her. She got into the car and drove away. He went back to his desk.

He sat for a long time, his head in his hands. He thought earlier in the day that he had reached his nadir, but his despair now was deeper than anything he had ever experienced. What the hell was he thinking of? He had made an utter fool of himself. There was no doubt in his own mind that he was no longer capable of making coherent judgements; no longer capable of making balanced choices. It was time he made a decision about his future.

He heard sounds of people moving about. The early arrivals were in the theatre preparing for the performance. He took his coat from the corner stand and saw her black file on the desk. He touched it lightly, put on his coat and left the office.

CHAPTER ELEVEN

Mack took Emma's arm as they left the restaurant and crossed the street to their car. He waited for a break in the traffic and forced his way into the mainstream.

He looked at his watch. 'We have just enough time before we meet Carter at his home.' He glanced at a street sign and turned left. 'I think we're losing sight of our primary assignment. Finding Amy.'

'Right. Let Sivo find the murderer. We'll find Amy.'

'I'd like to drive out to see Howard Bruneau at Château La Brède.'

Emma looked at him inquiringly. 'Because he went out at the same time as our intruder at Crab Island?'

'No. Because Carter said the Bruneau girl was Amy's close friend. I'm wondering where she would hole up if she was running.' He braked for a pedestrian who ran out in front of him. 'Blasted idiot!' They were silent as they nosed through the downtown traffic. They passed the theatre which was in a street off

Bayside, a long busy boulevard of elegant boutiques, curio shops and half a dozen shopping malls. The centre island was lined with coconut-palms and hibiscus-shrubs. Pedestrians in garments of every style and hue were noisy testimony to the effectiveness of the tourist board's marketing strategy.

Mack drove on into Mountain Drive, the road to Hungry Mountain. Beyond the mountain the road continued to Sentenille, Bougainville and Largo Point, three small fishing villages to the north of the island. Carter House was on a cul-de-sac that forked left just before the mountain. It was a road of smallholdings and half a dozen cottages. The Carter house was the last property on the road. As they approached, they saw a distinctive green and yellow Pascua police vehicle parked on the verge. A smartly uniformed policeman stepped into the road and held up his hand. Mack stopped just before the gate which had been left open for them.

The officer was painfully polite. 'So sorry to delay you, sir, but could you please tell me what paper you are from?'

Emma leaned forward. 'We are guests here, officer.'

He smiled. 'And your names please?'

'Emma Olsen and Colin McGlashan.'

'And which are you, madam?'

Emma smiled disarmingly. 'Well, officer,

I'm not Colin and he's not Emma. So what do you think?'

'Of course, madam. I'm sorry.' He smiled, made a note on his pad, and waved them on.

Mack growled. 'I'm not Colin! What a fatuous remark.' He put the car into gear. 'Did you have to embarrass the poor man?'

Emma pouted. 'Boy. Not a man. A polite and charming, good-looking boy.'

'Nevertheless you embarrassed him. Now if you don't behave yourself, I'll write a full report for Teig and Grampa.'

She smiled sweetly. 'Yea, Daddy Dear.'

Mack snorted. 'And that'll cost you another black mark.'

'Snitch!'

Mack laughed and stopped the car in front of the house. Blaine's car was already in its slot in the garages.

Mrs Garland greeted them cheerfully and added: 'You must both be exhausted; out all day with only a picnic basket.'

Emma smiled at her. 'We had tea at a hotel before we left the city.' Mrs Garland looked disappointed. Emma said quickly: 'But I know Mack would like something.' Mack grimaced, but smiled when Mrs Garland looked at him.

Mrs Garland beamed. 'I'll bring a tray to the study. Mr Carter is expecting you there.'

'Thank you, Mrs Garland.' As she turned to go, Emma said: 'Did Mr Carter bring the picnic basket back?'

'Yes dear. I took it into the scullery.'

They found Blaine standing with his back to the door, staring at the mountain. Misty traces feathered the summit, and the occasional gusts of wind held a baleful note. It would be a wild night. Emma wondered where Amy was and whether she was somewhere safe. The thought depressed her.

Carter sighed and turned.

'Please sit down.'

Emma sat on the sofa and Mack took the big chair. There was no sign of the photographs. When they were comfortable, Carter sat behind his desk. He was silent for a long time. The clock ticked away the passing seconds until his anguish poured out in a whisper: 'I didn't know.'

Mack shifted uncomfortably, but while his was the masculine reaction, Emma said:

'Of course you didn't. How could you know?' Her voice held a note of sympathy.

He shook his head. 'No. I should have known. The signs were all there. At least four of my company were involved.' He stood up angrily and walked to the window. With his back to them he said: 'They will say that they were only in the group pictures and were unaware of . . .'

Alarmed, Mack asked: 'You're going to confront them?'

Carter turned. 'Of course. I have to. How could they do this?'

'No. No and no.' Mack was vehement. 'The photos must be given to Sivo first, and he must be allowed time to slot the whole miserable affair into his investigation.' He watched Carter slump into his chair. 'I know with absolute certainty that Juliet was killed because of her involvement in whatever happened at Crab Island.' He leaned forward. 'No one must know that those photos have been found. You must give them to Sivo. As far as we know, besides us, only one other person knows that those photos are not still in the attic at Crab Island. You must let Sivo have that advantage.'

Emma nodded her approval. 'Mack's right. They must be given to the inspector, and the sooner the better.'

Carter protested. 'You said you would help me.'

Emma said quietly. 'To find Amy. Not to find a killer or to get involved with the people in those pictures.'

Carter threw up his hands. 'I'm sorry. I'm confused. To me they are the same thing. Somehow Amy's disappearance, Crab Island and the murder are linked.'

Emma stood up and walked to the window. 'Of course they are.' Carter's anguish began to disturb her. She looked across the kitchen garden towards the trees and the foothills beyond.

Mack looked at Emma and then at Blaine.

'If we look at one of the problems we might see a weapon to prise open one of the other two.'

Blaine frowned. 'I don't understand.'

'Give me the photographs and a writing pad.'

Emma heard a drawer open. In the silence that followed, she saw Mrs Garland appear from the trees with a full garbage bag. She passed through the vegetable garden and disappeared into the kitchen. The sun was low, disappearing behind the mountain, shadowing the eastern slopes of the hills. A horse whinnied and she caught the odours from the stables. As a wave of homesickness swept over her she turned and went back to the sofa.

Mack sorted through the pile of about fifty photographs. When he had put aside a smaller pile, he handed the rest to Carter.

'Put those away.' He placed the photographs one at a time along the desk. 'As you identify the people you see here, I will number the prints and Emma will record the names.' He handed the pad to her. 'But first, do you know who this is?' He placed his finger on a stunningly beautiful woman in a group in front of the print of Seurat's *Models*.

Carter examined the print closely. 'She's familiar.' He looked up thoughtfully. 'Yes. Juliet brought her to the theatre last week. ̓ and another woman were Juliet's g̓ theatre. They only stayed untiʼ

interval and left to dine at a restaurant in town where Haig and Helen Summers joined them after the show.' He made a face. 'She said the play bored them. That was the only time I saw them.' He looked quizzically at Mack. 'What is so significant about her?'

'Both Emma and I have seen her before. What's her name?'

'Oh hell, I should remember.' He paused. 'I'm usually good at names.' He agonized for a moment. 'Robin, I think. No, Roberta; that's it. Roberta. I'm sure of it.'

'You don't know any more about her?'

'No. I only saw her once. Juliet's guests come and go like chaff in the wind.' He added bitterly: 'She used the theatre and my actors to socialize.'

Mack looked at the girl in the photo. 'It's a start. Now these others.'

He numbered a second photograph and held it up.

Carter took it from him. 'Helen Summers. Ken Haig and Robert Hansen.'

'I know the first two are actors. Who is Hansen?'

'He's a banker from San Francisco. He was here for a week a few months ago. Riley brought him to the theatre.'

'Married?'

'I don't know. If he is, his wife wasn't with him.' He paused and sat back and looked at ¹ie window. He looked at Mack. 'I remember now. He was here for a banking seminar. Riley secured it for Pascua when he heard they were looking for a venue.' He looked at the next photograph and placed a finger on one of the group. 'He was also here for that seminar.' He shook his head. 'I don't remember hearing his name.'

Mack passed picture after picture to Carter until Emma had numbered forty-three in the first two batches. Mack sighed and sat back. 'Now we have only this last group. Are you up to it?'

Carter had a hunted look. 'It has to be done.' He sat back. 'Yes. I'm up to it.'

'Right. Let's begin.'

Emma stood up and put the pad on the table. 'I'm sorry, Mack. I've seen a couple of these already. I don't want to see them again. I'm going to the kitchen to beg Mrs Garland for a sandwich.' She went out. I need a sandwich like I need a hole in the head. she thought. Still, it's better than looking at that lot again.

She went quietly down the passage to Amy's room, and opened the door. She looked in the wardrobes, but the item she was looking for was not there. She found it on the floor in the bathroom, peered inside to be sure it was the article she sought, nodded with satisfaction and left the room closing the door behind her.

While she was engaged in her private pursuit the men were carefully cataloguing and numbering the photographs. The subjects in the last batch were all nudes, both male and female, but when a woman was clearly visible, the man's face was obscured. When a man was recognizable, only part of a woman's legs and arms were visible. In eight of the batch of twelve photographs, Carter identified the recognizable subjects. Mack numbered the last one, wrote the name on the pad and added the prints to the first two batches.

Mack tapped the pad. 'So what we have here are three men and five women in what used to be called *flagrante delicto.*'

Carter said drily: 'Still is as far as I know.' He gathered up the prints and placed them in the right top drawer of his desk. There was a long silence. He stood up and went to the window that was dark now with the mantle of night. The wind gusted and no sky was visible. Mack wondered what he was looking at; probably the torn and wasted years.

Mrs Garland appeared in the doorway with the tea-tray. She placed it on the small table. 'Dinner will be ready at half past seven, and I must say how nice it is to have you home for a change, Mr Carter.'

She smiled at Mack and went out.

Mack watched her go. 'She's remarkably cheerful today. She was almost singing when she greeted us just now.'

Carter smiled. 'Mrs Garland? Singing? Never.'

Mack shrugged. He walked to the window and peered out into the darkness. 'Devoted to Amy, was she?'

'Amy could have been a daughter.'

'Umm. Strange.' He turned from the window. 'Under the circumstances, decidedly strange.'

Carter shrugged. 'I've learnt that there is no standard one can look for in reactions to a particular set of circumstances.'

Mack smiled. 'I hear the convictions of a stage director.'

Carter looked embarrassed. 'Sorry. I get a little professorial when I get on to the things I know best.'

Mack said apologetically: 'I didn't mean to be disparaging.'

Carter shrugged off the apology. 'I know that. But you're quite right. Mrs Garland is remarkably cheerful.'

Mack moved to the door. 'I must shower and change for dinner or Mrs Garland will be less than happy. I expect Emma is ahead of me.' He went out.

CHAPTER TWELVE

Ethel Sivo looked out of the window from the house in Palm Avenue, just off South Shore Drive. She could see the top of the hill, but there was still no sign of Joe or Sheldon. Cooking supper for a son and husband, neither of whom considered punctuality more important than whatever they were doing at seven o'clock, could have been a frustrating experience for most women, but not for Ethel Sivo, who was placid and long-suffering. She went into the kitchen, spotless, white and willow-pattern, switched off the stove and went through to the living-room.

Her husband loved this room. She'd known he would when she furnished it. Two large, deep-cushioned sofas faced one another, with three flanking armchairs placed strategically around the room to take advantage of the enormous picture window with its view of the sea beyond the white sands of Southern Beach.

She never regretted her decision to choose Joe Sivo and Pascua over her village in Yorkshire, though at first she missed the essentially British institutions: The Proms, listening to the BBC on the wireless, going with her dad to watch Leeds United playing at home and seeing the Cup Final on the telly. The separation from her native land would have been more difficult if there had been a family to go back to, but she had been alone after her father died. She had been surprised at the size of her inheritance and had decided to invest some on a once in a lifetime holiday in the Pacific, but when she met Joe her journey ended abruptly in Pascua.

When Sivo met her she was feisty, slim, and pretty. In spite of the passing years and greying hair, she was still tiny and pretty, but she sometimes lamented the slight thickening of her hips. Only this morning she had looked in the mirror and sighed at the loss of her figure.

Joe had been sceptical. 'Nonsense. You're as slim as you were twenty-five years ago. There's not an ounce of fat there.'

She had pouted. 'Only a policeman would refuse to accept facts without proof.' She paused. 'I'll weigh myself.' She had smiled mischievously. 'A hundred on the result.'

'I know you. You'll cheat.'

'I'll take a polygraph test.'

'No good. I'll only accept visual evidence.'

She had said sternly. 'Any more indecent remarks and I'll call a copper.'

Yesterday, she had asked him with mock tearfulness why their marriage was a failure. 'Look at all our friends,' she said. 'Great marriages. Always quarrelling, fighting and threatening divorce. I should give you a black eye now and then.'

When he had thrown a cushion at her, she had beamed happily. 'At last. Grounds for divorce.'

Their badinage, always lively, always affectionate and good-natured was energetic but never bruising. It was the adhesive that helped bind them in a happy marriage.

She heard a car in their driveway. A door

slammed and Sheldon came inside. He kissed his mother quickly on the cheek.

'What's to eat?' He took off his coat. 'Is Pop home?'

'Not yet.' She turned on the stove. 'If he's not here in fifteen minutes we'll start without him.' Sheldon went into the living-room.

Joe Sivo arrived just as Ethel was serving. He seemed preoccupied. She watched him, sensing that he was troubled. She passed him a plate.

'Tough day?'

He nodded. 'It's always tough when good friends are involved in an inquiry.' He looked at her with approval. 'You were right about her.' He jabbed a fork into a roast potato. 'Yes, you were right—again.'

'This time I really wish I had been wrong. Juliet had a funny life style but Blaine didn't deserve what happened.'

Sheldon said. 'And I fixed three cars today.' He pulled the gravy boat closer. 'But before I tell you about them . . .'

Joe laughed. 'I did it again. I made the rule and I keep breaking it.' He raised a hand. 'Right. No more shop talk at meal-times.'

Sheldon nodded approvingly. 'You didn't break the rule. That lady who lives with us did it by asking you about your day.' He stood up, kissed her on the top of her head and went to the sideboard for a water-glass.

Ethel flashed him a smile. 'And how was

your day?'

Joe said: 'You're incorrigible.'

Later, as Ethel began to take the plates to the kitchen, Joe leaned back in his chair and said: 'I want you to look at a photo of a plaster cast. It's a tyre-print.' He stood up. 'It's in my briefcase. Forensics will look at it tomorrow, but you may identify the make.'

He returned with three ten-by-twelve prints. Sheldon looked at them carefully one at a time, his dark eyebrows meeting in a thoughtful frown.

He looked up. 'Michelin.' He tapped the photo. 'The footprint makes it a one-seven-five. Probably a seventy-by-thirteen.' His frown relaxed. 'The tread is MXV3A.'

Joe took the print and beamed. 'Fantastic.' He slipped the photographs back into the briefcase. 'Want to join the force? I'll take you on as our tyre expert.'

Sheldon shook his head vehemently. 'No thanks.'

Ethel put her head in the door. 'I heard that. I've got a first lien on that boy. At the moment he's my dish-washer. Get in here, you,' she said severely.

Sheldon sighed. 'What's the pay like in the force?'

*   *   *

Sivo put on his coat and looked at his watch.

'It's half past eight. I should be home by ten.'

Ethel handed him his briefcase. 'I don't know why this can't wait until morning.'

He tapped the briefcase. 'Now that the lad has identified the tyre-tracks for me, I want to put someone on it.' He smiled.

'Besides, I want to light a fire under young Williams. He told me forensics could take up to three days to find a match in their files.'

Ethel shook her head disapprovingly. 'Go easy on that boy. Stop badgering him.'

Sivo growled. 'About time he grew up and married that girl of his.'

She pulled his head down and kissed his cheek. 'Just because you're trapped in a loveless marriage with a repulsive old harridan, you want everyone else to be unhappy.'

'Don't worry,' he said darkly. 'It won't last for ever—I've got plans for you.' He hugged her tightly and went out to the car.

The Bay was on his right as he took the long curve on South Shore Drive. Across the water Pascua Bay glinted with hundreds of shifting reflections from the lights in tall buildings on Bayside. The gusting wind from the ocean carried with it the omnipresent tang of ozone. As a boy, when the damp scent of the sea was in his nostrils, he had had the romantic belief that angels were blowing zephyrs from across the sea; the same breezes that had brought his ancestors to the islands from the western

154

shores. There was a time when he had told Ethel about his notion. It was on the moonlit deck of a cruise liner. She had looked into his face, hugged him, and knew that he was the man she would love for the rest of her life.

Williams met him at the hotel entrance.

The inspector frowned. 'Been waiting long?'

'Just got here.'

'Let's go up, then.'

The foyer was almost empty. A group of formally dressed couples were chatting as they drifted through a dining-room door which was flanked by a card on a stand announcing an architectural conference.

As the lift began to glide up to the tenth floor, Sivo said: 'When are you getting married?'

Williams gave him a startled glance. Then he smiled inwardly. 'I see too many unhappy, middle-aged people to do anything silly.' He paused. 'Why do you ask?'

Sivo shrugged. 'Ethel keeps asking me,' he lied.

'Is that why she said I shouldn't take any notice if you badgered me about it?'

Sivo shifted uncomfortably. 'Said that, did she?'

To Williams' relief, the lift doors opened with a pneumatic hush. A young uniformed constable saluted as they stepped out.

'Don't salute me, lad. I'm not a bloody general.' He paused and stared at the young

155

man. 'Forrest isn't it?'

'Yes sir. Sorry sir.' The constable coughed apologetically. 'There's someone with her.'

'Who?' Sivo was plainly irritated.

Behind him, Williams hid a smile. He surmised that he was responsible for the inspector's ill-humour. Serves him bloody right, he thought. Married indeed!

'It's that lawyer fellow. Jonathon Burns.' He coughed nervously. 'And the girl's mother.'

'Well what are you doing out here?'

'He said they wasn't to be disturbed. He said it was a conference.'

'Conference? I'll give him conference!'

Sivo pushed open the door and marched into the room. Three pairs of eyes looked up, startled. Jonathon Burns, in a neat grey suit and maroon tie was sitting at the table opposite Sylvia Phillips. Gerda Martin occupied the easy chair at the window. The bedroom door was open revealing an untidy assortment of clothing on the bed and two suitcases on the floor.

Burns stood up, paced to the window and looked at Sivo through his gold-rimmed spectacles. 'Ah Sivo. Just in time. Mrs Phillips will be leaving on the Sydney flight in an hour. I was about to call you at home.'

Sivo swallowed his anger. He matched the lawyer's urbanity. 'Mrs Phillips is in protective custody and will remain here until this investigation is complete.'

Burns was polite but firm. 'Now Joe, you know you can't get away with that.' He went to the papers on the table. 'Both Mrs Phillips and her mother have described their movements last night.' He picked up a sheet of grey legal paper. He smiled disarmingly at Sivo. 'We can do this the hard way if you wish, but Judge Vicente won't be very pleased to be visited at this hour.' He replaced the paper. 'If you're called on to show cause, what have you got?'

Before Sivo could speak, Gerda Martin spat venomously:

'This is nothing but harassment. No one in his right mind could believe that my daughter murdered Juliet Carter.'

Burns attempted to stop her, but her anger was a spark that fuelled her hatred of the policeman. She continued over the lawyer's protestations:

'It's disgraceful. How can you accuse her of strangling Mrs Carter, ransacking the house, wrecking the bedroom, and smashing a mirror and vase all in a matter of five minutes?'

Sivo looked at Sylvia. Her eyes were red-rimmed from lack of sleep. Burns tilted his head, a mannerism Sivo had seen many times in the courtroom.

'Just why were you holding her, Joe?'

'Because she hasn't told the whole truth about her involvement with Juliet Carter.' He walked to the window and turned his back on the room. 'She denied going to Crab Island but

157

there is clear evidence that she had been there.'

Burns smiled and sighed patiently. 'Come on, Joe. What has Crab Island got to do with a murder at the house at Hungry Mountain? Mrs Phillips has admitted to me that she lied. Clearly she was reluctant to be linked with the wild parties at the island.' He looked at Sylvia. 'Go and pack.' The girl went into the bedroom.

Sergeant Williams watched the exchanges as a spectator would watch a tennis match. He waited for a huge smashing volley from the inspector; a *coup de grâce* that would demolish the lawyer and leave him floundering; but it never came. Instead Sivo nodded resignedly.

'She can go, but if I need her, just remember we have an extradition treaty with the United Kingdom.'

'Always a dash of melodrama, Joe.' Burns gathered his papers and stuffed them into the briefcase. 'It's not like you to give up so easily.' He smiled. 'Sure you haven't got something up your sleeve?'

Sivo looked at the girl packing in the bedroom. 'Just make sure she gets that Sydney plane.'

He went out. Williams followed him, closing the door behind him. Sivo looked at the young constable waiting in the corridor. 'What the hell are you still doing here? Go home to mummy.'

Williams winked at the young man who

smiled ruefully and followed them to the lift.

*   *   *

Blaine Carter sat at the head of a mahogany dining-room table that seated eighteen. Emma sat on his left with Mack opposite her. Only the end of the table was set for dinner.

Whether it was the informality, or whether Blaine had accepted Mack's assurances that Amy would soon be returned to him, he appeared to be more relaxed though still somewhat depressed.

As she looked down the expanse of bare table, Emma imagined the scene on special occasions, with the silverware gleaming, serving dishes steaming and guests in black ties and expensive gowns chattering to each other between elaborate courses. If Amy's infrequent letters were to be believed, her stepmother's fortnightly dinner-parties were attended by politicians, actors, bankers and celebrities who visited the islands. The large sideboard behind her and the two credenzas against the wall opposite her, testified to the elaborate nature of the service on those occasions. Over and between the two credenzas hung a print of *The Night Watch*. The closed curtains covered the entire wall opposite the door.

Emma pushed a potato to the side of her plate and sighed. 'I'm afraid I'm not very hungry.' She looked at Blaine as she placed her knife and fork on the plate. 'Would you mind if I ask Mrs Garland a few questions after dinner?'

Blaine's surprise replaced the dispirited look on his face. 'Mrs Garland? Of course.' He looked puzzled. 'About Juliet? Amy?' He looked across the dinner-table at Mack. 'Do you think she knows something pertinent?'

Emma shook her head. 'I don't know, I'd like to try something.'

Blaine nodded resignedly. 'Anything that will help find Amy.'

Mack, who was privy to Emma's strategy, put his serviette aside and stood up. 'Whatever you do, don't do it here. This is her domain, the place where she is most comfortable. Do it in the study.'

'You make it sound like an interrogation.'

Emma said quickly: 'It's not an interrogation, but Mack's suggestion makes sense if she is withholding something.'

Blaine shrugged. 'If you think it will help.' It was obvious that he thought the whole idea was ludicrous.

At that moment Mrs Garland appeared from the kitchen. Blaine said: 'When you're finished here, please come to the study. We would like you to help us with something.'

The housekeeper looked apprehensively at Mack as though anticipating what was to come. She nodded silently and went back to

160

the kitchen.

It was more than half an hour before the housekeeper joined them in the study, an interval which Emma used to brief Mack and Blaine on her assumptions. As Mrs Garland entered Emma took her arm and guided her to the armchair on the right of the fireplace. Mack sat at the desk, while Emma stood against the curtained window. Blaine sat on the straight-backed chair on the left of the desk. For a moment no one spoke. The loud ticking of the clock underscored the silence. Mrs Garland moved her shoulders and glanced at her employer. She looked frail and defenceless. Blaine smiled encouragingly.

Emma spoke quietly. 'We hope you will help us, Mrs Garland.'

'I'll do all I can. What is it you want to know?' She spoke with assurance, but her hunched shoulders reflected her nervousness.

'Where did Amy sleep last night?'

Mrs Garland looked surprised but Emma knew it was feigned. 'I'm sure I don't know. She left after I retired.'

Mack shook his head. 'That won't do. We know she rushed over to your apartment when she found Mrs Carter.' He was guessing, but he knew it was the only theory that fitted the facts.

Mrs Garland looked at her employer. Blaine saw the appeal in her eyes, but he knew they had to learn what she knew if they were to

161

find Amy.

She looked at Emma. 'I never saw her after I went to bed.'

Emma sighed with exasperation. 'Amy may be in grave danger. We have to find her if we want her safe. We know that Amy is alone and frightened. She isn't thinking rationally and we have to find her to protect her.' She paused, waiting for the housekeeper to speak, but Mrs Garland looked at the floor and remained silent.

'Please, Mrs Garland. If we don't find her soon, we may never see her again.'

Another long pause.

'She must have seen the killer, and she must be terribly afraid of him, otherwise she would not have disappeared.'

When she looked up, the woman's cheeks glistened with tears.

'What makes you think I saw her?'

Mack recognized the classic question of the guilty. Not a denial, but the exploratory route to discover what the interrogator knew. It was time to show her the extent of their knowledge. He nodded to Emma.

'You see, Mrs Garland, earlier this evening I saw you when you came from the trees carrying what I thought was a garbage bag. Then I asked myself why you would be carrying a garbage bag *towards* the house.' She took a pace from the window. 'Then, while I watched you go to the kitchen, I realized it wasn't garbage you were carrying, but a black tent-bag. I saw that the thing you were carrying was too regular to be garbage.' She walked behind the big chair. 'You see, I have one at home, only mine is green.' Emma went back to the window. 'You hid it in Amy's bathroom until you could return it to where it is normally stored.' There was a long pause. The men watched silently as Mrs Garland lifted a tearful face, turning pleading eyes to her employer.

All at once Emma felt a stab of pity for her, and shame at her own role in badgering the elderly woman; but without her, they would never find Amy. Emma was convinced that Amy was irrational and afraid and probably in shock as anyone would be after finding a parent murdered and, she surmised, seeing the killer. Clearly if the person she had seen was someone she knew, her shock would be all the more traumatic.

Impulsively she went to the armchair, and sat on the arm. She put her hands on the frail shoulders, and said kindly: 'We remembered that Mr Carter said Amy loved that mountain. He said she knew all the trails and often took her tent and camped out there.'

Mrs Garland dabbed at her eyes and looked directly at Blaine.

'I'm sorry, Mr Carter. Amy asked me to help her. She was desperately afraid. She said she had to hide for a few days. She said no one would believe her if she told what she had

163

seen.'

Emma stood up and walked to the window. She felt a huge sense of relief. In a few seconds they would know where Amy was; but her relief was short-lived.

Mrs Garland hesitated. When she spoke, her voice was firmer. 'She was only in the woods for about an hour before she changed her mind. At about eleven o'clock she came to my apartment and said she had to find somewhere safer, but she refused to say where she was going.' She paused, looked at Emma and then at Mack. 'Only that she knew where she could be safe for a few days.' She added: 'Then she asked me to fetch the bag from where she had left it, and drove off at about half past eleven.'

Carter looked drawn and ill. He said: 'Did you go into Juliet's bedroom?'

'Oh yes, but when I realized there was nothing I could do I went back to my room.' She paused. 'I thought of calling the police, but decided to give Amy time to get away to where she felt she would be safe. Then I heard you come in and stayed where I was until the police came.'

Emma realized what a terrible dilemma had faced Mrs Garland. Yet her love for Amy had given her the strength and courage to act in what she thought were Amy's interests.

Carter stood up. He said to Mack: 'Are you fiinished?'

Mack nodded. 'Thank you, Mrs Garland.' His voice softened. 'You've been very brave. I know what it is to have a friend like you, and how much courage it took to act as you did.'

As she stood up Blaine said: 'I'm glad you were there to help my daughter. Thank you for what you did.' He led her to the door. 'We'll find her and bring her home. I promise.'

Mack stood up. 'We'd better move quickly.'

Blaine said firmly. 'If you know where she is, I'm coming too.'

'No. You stay here in case she comes back. She's running like a frightened hare. She is completely irrational. Fear and shock has taken over and there is no knowing what she will do next.'

'Where is she?'

'I think she is at the Bruneau château, but there is no certainty that she will stay there if she feels threatened.'

'Do you think she is in danger?'

Mack hesitated. He was unwilling to cause Carter any more anxiety, but he should know the truth. 'I believe she is. I'm sure we are being followed by someone who believes we know where she is.'

Emma went to the door. 'I want to shower and change. What was the name of Amy's friend. The Bruneau girl?'

'Fran. Short for Françoise.'

Mack said: 'Expect us back by midnight. I hope we can bring you good news.'

CHAPTER THIRTEEN

Sivo strode from the lift and turned left into the small comfortable coffee-lounge off the main dining-room. Sergeant Williams and Constable Forrest followed him to a table at the back of the lounge.

Forrest fidgeted nervously, unsure of whether to sit or remain standing.

'Do you need me tonight, sir?'

Sivo looked at him speculatively.

'Yes,' Sivo growled. 'I'll give you a chance to redeem yourself. But for heaven's sake sit down if you want a cup of coffee. Then you can go off with Sergeant Williams.'

Williams nodded surreptitiously to the young man who sat reluctantly in the third chair.

'Thank you, sir.'

Williams said: 'We could have stayed upstairs and called room service.'

'Don't be bloody facetious,' Sivo snapped irritably. 'That facility is reserved for Pascua's pampered felons.' A waiter appeared at his right. 'These gentlemen are drinking coffee. I'll have a pot of tea.' The waiter disappeared.

Williams couldn't resist a little provocation. 'May I have tea too?'

'I'm paying, so you'll have coffee.'

Williams decided he had reached the limit

of his luck. He retired gracefully. 'Thanks. Coffee will do fine.'

Constable Forrest said hastily: 'Coffee's fine for me too.' If the inspector had suggested castor oil he would have agreed.

The three men were silent until the waiter returned with their order.

The inspector took a first sip and grimaced. 'Why is it wives make better tea than hotels?' He took another sip. 'Right, Sergeant. This is what I want you to do. Go down to that photographer and wait for me there. Take Forrest here with you and secure the premises until I get a search warrant.' He looked fiercely at the young man. 'Think you can guard the place without letting a battery of lawyers swarm all over it?'

'I'm sorry, sir. Mr Burns demanded . . .'

'It's all right, lad. It wasn't your fault. Just make sure no one goes into Bellamy's until I get there with a warrant.'

Williams was shocked. 'Tonight, sir?'

'Unless you want to sleep here until morning.'

'Isn't it a bit late, sir?'

'Late for what?' The inspector drained his cup. 'It's only nine o'clock.' He placed the cup and saucer on the table and said blandly. 'I suppose you want to rush off and propose to that young lady of yours.' He shook his head. 'You can do that first thing tomorrow. After you've called in at forensics and given them

167

this information on that tyre-cast.' He passed a slip of paper across the table. 'Then ask them if they can tell us how many sets of fingerprints they lifted from Juliet Carter's bedroom.' He smiled grimly. 'And if they tell you five clear sets, I'll buy you a big balloon. I want them compared with Mrs Carter's, Mr Carter's, Mrs Garland's and Amy Carter's.'

Williams made a note. He looked up. 'Which team is looking for Amy Carter?'

'Amy Carter? What do we want with Amy Carter? They can lift any number of prints from her bedroom for comparison.'

'But you said, and I quote: "a full-scale search is under way for Amy Carter". I heard you say it.' Williams was becoming irritated, but he was careful to remain respectful.

Inspector Sivo smiled indulgently. 'You really must learn to know when I'm serious and when I'm putting a stick in the hornets' nest.'

'So you were putting a stick in the hornets' nest when you said that?'

The inspector sighed patiently. 'That Olsen girl and her brother . . .'

'He's her stepfather.' Williams could have bitten off his tongue. Sivo was needling him and he had fallen for it. The inspector knew damned well she was his stepdaughter.

'Whatever. Anyway they're running around looking for Amy Carter. It's keeping them busy and out of mischief.' He stood up. 'Amy

Carter is in no danger. She's at the Bruneaus'.'

'How do you know?'

'There are nine people in that house. Too many to keep a secret.'

For once the inspector's confidence was misplaced.

*   *   *

The wind had dropped, the clouds had drifted out to sea and as they drove out of the gates the mountain loomed high against a sky that prickled with stars. There was no moon but a glow on the horizon heralded a moonlit night. The air was fresh with a blend of fragrances that grew out of the woods and mingled with the ozone-scented sea-breezes.

At the junction they turned north to skirt the mountain and dropped down to the central plain where sugar-plantations filled every acre of arable land. The tall stalks crowded the narrow road so that at times the headlights were confined to the road before them. At the top of a small rise they saw a glow from a cluster of large buildings. On the clear night air their senses were assailed by the rumble of machinery and the sweet smell of crushed sugar cane. They passed a junction where a dirt road branched to the right and left of the main road. In the distance they could see the twinkling lights of a small settlement. A signpost appeared in the headlights with one arm pointing left to *Les Buka* and the other to *Sentenille.*

Mack paused at the fork and looked in the rear-view mirror. Emma looked behind them. 'What is it?'

It was a minute before he spoke. He remained staring in the mirror. 'I'm certain there was a car behind us. He picked us up as we left the mountain.'

Although she respected Mack's acumen, she looked doubtful. 'It could have been quite innocent.'

He shook his head. 'I don't think so. He had his lights on until he closed up, then he drove without lights. I saw the car against the sky when he topped a rise behind us.' He waited for a moment longer. Then he put the car in gear. 'He's not there now.'

They took the right fork and a few minutes later they were passing the small village of Sentenille where only a single light glowed at the edge of a cliff. They heard the muted rumble of the surf against the rocks far below.

A few minutes later they topped a slight rise to see the lights of Bougainville below them. It was a moderate-sized village which sloped down to the sea from a high point about a hundred feet above the beach. Emma wished they had come in daylight. The single main street, which was parallel to the sea, was cut across by several short lanes. Houses crowded one another and the pervasive odour of fish testified to its major industry.

Mack slowed the car at the entrance to the main street. Emma pointed to the top of the hill where a house, bigger than anything they had seen on the island, was ablaze with light. It looked down over the village and the sea. Mack turned in to the first lane and pointed the car at the hilltop. The château was bigger than it appeared from below but to Mack's eyes it was not even a miniature of the French original. There was a castellated structure and a round tower and spire, but there the similarity ended. A bright light at the front of the house illuminated a heavy wooden double door, that would admit any vehicle under ten feet high. A conventional door was let into the left side of the main door. An oversized bell-push was fixed to the smaller door.

Emma followed Mack from the car. He thumbed the bell-push and heard the distant peal of fairly large chimes. After a wait of a few minutes the smaller door was opened by a young man who looked at them curiously without speaking.

'Mr Bruneau?'

'Not guilty.'

'We would like to see Mr Bruneau. I'm McGlashan and this is Mrs Emma Olsen.'

'Wait here.' The door was closed.

Emma looked at Mack. 'Charming.'

After a short wait the door was opened by a young, pretty, black-haired girl. She smiled at

Emma.

'You must be Emma. I'm Gerry Bruneau. We heard you were visiting.'

They heard a voice from inside the house. 'Who is it, Geraldine?'

'Friends of the Carters', Mother. They have come to see Father.'

'Well bring them in. Don't keep them standing out there.' The girl smiled and opened the door wide. 'You heard Mother. Come in.'

They were met by a tall, elegant woman dressed in a stylish grey dress and black pumps. The hall in which she greeted them was furnished with spindly eighteenth century French pieces. There was a half-round table against the right wall and a writing-desk on the left. Through a wide arch they could see similar pieces in the living-room beyond. The only exception was a solid monk's bench against the wall that divided the hall from the living-room.

The woman extended a hand and her greeting was flavoured with a strong French accent.

'I am Mrs Bruneau. Welcome to La Brède.'

The dim light from the sconces threw a shadow on her face which made it difficult to read her expression, but Emma thought she detected a hint of anxiety in her greeting. Emma looked at her closely. She was the quintessential French expatriate; elegant, cultured and sad, with memories of her native land influencing every decision so that her new life was layered under a coating of longing for what was left behind. Her kind never adapted to change.

Mack returned the greeting for both of them, whereupon Mrs Bruneau led the way through the arch to a comfortable living-room. Gerry followed them and immediately walked across the room to a sofa and joined the young man who had opened the door to them. There were two other young women in the room, both seated on sofas and each attended by a young man.

Mack glanced at Emma and murmured: 'To quote Jane Austen, *he is not in the least addicted to locking up his daughters.*'

Emma hid a smile. Mrs Bruneau introduced them to each of the young people in the room. Françoise was not one of them.

Mack frowned. 'You have four daughters?'

Mrs Bruneau smiled. 'How clever of you. Yes, I have four daughters, but Françoise is away in Sydney at the moment.' She paused. 'Amy must have told you that Françoise was her special friend.'

She's quick, Emma thought. She shook her head. 'No, not Amy. Mr Carter.'

Mack looked at Geraldine. 'You knew we were on Pascua. How?'

There was a silence that dragged on for an uncomfortable minute. Mrs Bruneau said quickly: 'When we were told by a friend of the shocking events at the Carter home, she told us of your presence then.'

Mack murmured quietly: 'I wonder how she knew?'

Emma smiled disarmingly at Geraldine. 'Did Amy know of our arrival?'

'Oh no. She had left before . . .' She stopped.

No one spoke, then Mrs Bruneau said: 'If you wish to see Mr Bruneau, I'll take you to him.' She signalled that they should follow her as she led the way through the dining-room to the opposite side of the house where a glass double-door opened on to a *lanai* under a bower which trailed bougainvillea and honeysuckle.

Mr Bruneau was a dim figure reclining in one of the half-dozen loungers scattered around the porch. Mrs Bruneau said: 'Friends of Amy to see you, Howard. I'll leave them with you while I arrange refreshments.' She paused. 'I'm sorry, we don't serve liquor.' She went inside.

As he stood up to greet them, they saw a tall grey-haired man, lean, muscled and friendly. As he moved into the light of a single Chinese lantern, they saw he had the deep tan of one who spent his life in the sun.

'Welcome.' He pushed two loungers to make a semicircle with his own. 'Whatever you've come for, I refuse to discuss it, until

174

I've seen off the *Florida Queen*.' He gestured seawards where the lights of a cruise liner sparkled and shimmered across a sea that reflected the path of a rising moon. As they sat, awed to silence by the magnificence of the display, the liner passed across the moonglow to disappear around the headland to the north.

Bruneau sighed. 'I never tire of seeing them. There are at least four a week, and sometimes I drive up to Largo Point to watch from there.' He gave an embarrassed laugh. 'My girls call it juvenile.' Emma reflected on the lack of a French accent, though she heard the occasional Polynesian inflection.

Mack smiled. 'There are many things more juvenile.'

The night was balmy, with a slight, temperate breeze. They heard the muted sound of breakers on the reef and the soft dissonance of innumerable insects.

Bruneau sighed. 'I suppose you've come to find Amy Carter?'

Mack nodded. 'We have. And since you are being blunt about it, we know she came here late last night.'

Bruneau stood up and walked to the edge of the *lanai*. 'She did. But she isn't here now.'

Mack said brusquely: 'If you tell us where she is, we'll leave at once.' He had no time for those who played games with people's lives. 'She is in grave danger, Mr Bruneau; from herself and from the killer.'

Bruneau turned to face them, 'Oh come, Mr McGlashan. She is a little overwrought, naturally. Who wouldn't be in the circumstances? But as for being in danger from . . .'

'She is more than overwrought, Mr Bruneau, but I have no intention of debating the point. I want to know immediately where we can find her.'

Emma said quietly: 'Why are you evading the issue, Mr Bruneau? Surely Mr Carter should be told. He is extremely perturbed about her disappearance.'

Bruneau hesitated. 'I promised both Fran and Amy I would not divulge her whereabouts.'

Mack stood up impatiently. 'Is Fran with her?'

'They left together.'

'When? This morning?'

'Yes.'

'Where is Amy's car? Here?'

Bruneau nodded and sighed. 'It's hidden in Fran's garage. Under a tarpaulin.'

Mack spoke firmly. 'Do you realize that Amy is a suspect?'

'Rubbish. She wouldn't murder anyone.'

'It doesn't alter the fact that you can be charged for defeating the ends of justice.'

'Joe Sivo wouldn't throw that at me. He's a family friend.'

Emma said quietly: 'I have only known

176

Inspector Sivo for a short while, but I believe he is a dedicated, honest policeman. He will throw the book at you, regardless of your friendship.'

Bruneau moved uneasily to the lounger.

'She took Amy to Crab Island.'

Mack's voice rose angrily. 'And left her there alone? That was stupid and irresponsible.' Bruneau remained silent.

'Come on, Emma. We have to go.'

They walked out past a silent and subdued group. It was obvious that they had heard the altercation.

As he was about to start the car, Mack said: 'Didn't the Uva Point people say that Howard Bruneau took his boat out?'

'No. They said one of the boats was a private craft owned by Howard Bruneau. And they would not question a woman's voice reporting their destination. He could have been going out with one of his family.'

Mack grimaced. 'I've been taking too much at face value. I've been sloppy. It won't happen again.'

When Emma spoke, her voice was bleak. 'Amy must have been there when we arrived this morning.' Her voice rose. 'Why did she avoid us? Why did she hide?'

'She wasn't hiding from us. She was running away from the person who arrived just before we did.'

Emma nodded. 'And she presumed we were

part of the same group. She was probably somewhere deep in the bush.' She looked thoughtful. 'If we're going out there tonight, we should telephone Blaine.'

'There's a telephone-box in the main street. We'll call from there.'

Emma yawned. 'I hope I can stay awake.'

CHAPTER FOURTEEN

Blaine Carter sat in the library staring out across the foothills towards the mountain, his thoughts a maelstrom of conflicting emotions; paramount was his anxiety for Amy's safety but mingled with his distress were both regret and discomfiture at the way he had blurted out his innermost feelings to Rhoda Larkin. He expected to find her resignation on his desk in the morning. He wouldn't blame her. He had been insensitive and impetuous, but he could not reproach himself without a consideration of his state of mind. His vulnerability had breached the dyke of his reticence, revealing, to his own surprise, passions of which he was unaware until now.

He left the library and paced restlessly about the house while the implications of Juliet's death slowly and belatedly began to dawn on him. Hitherto shock, grief and anger had smothered any logical thought-process, leaving him numbed and apathetic. Now, slowly, he was aware of the emergence of a resolve that drew on the intensity he habitually brought to his work in the theatre. He realized suddenly that he should not have allowed Mack to sideline him into a passive role. He made for the study. He knew what he had to do.

The phone was ringing when he opened the door. He snatched up the receiver.

'Blaine?' It was Rhoda Larkin. Her voice was tremulous. Uncertain.

'Rhoda?' His spirits lifted.

'Blaine, I . . .' She hesitated. He waited, careful not to break into what he guessed was her resignation speech; or to embarrass her by giving her the impression that he was anticipating this moment.

Her first words startled him. 'I want to say how sorry I am that I walked out on you. It was heartless and unkind.' She paused. 'I'm finding this difficult.' Another pause. 'Oh damn. I'd better leave this until I see you in the office.'

Blaine sensed that if he let this moment pass he would always regret it. To lessen her discomfiture he took an oblique approach.

'I know I alarmed you today, and I realize now that I was completely out of line. It wasn't the place nor the time.'

'Oh no. It was only that I . . .' She stopped. 'Oh damn. Why is it that we who are always reading dialogue from a book find it so difficult to make ourselves understood?'

'Go on. You're doing fine.' He was smiling.

As though she sensed it, she said: 'You must find this amusing.'

He sobered. 'No. I understand completely.'

'Are you sure?'

'Absolutely. I know how embarrassed you must have felt at my own clumsiness. I expressed myself badly, but I meant every word.'

There was a long pause. When she spoke her voice was firmer.

'When I decided to telephone, I knew exactly what I wanted to say, but now it seems so—so much like dialogue from a bad play.'

There was another short silence. 'Oh hell. I'm going to say it anyway. When I stopped to think about what you said; about how you felt, I realized it was what I had dreamed about without believing it could ever happen.' Her voice dropped. She said softly: 'I've loved you for a long time, Blaine, but you were right. The time isn't appropriate. I believe we should put our feelings aside until the time is right. I just wanted you to know.'

Blaine's spirits were soaring, but he said simply: 'Thank you.'

'That's all I wanted to say. I'll be in the office as usual tomorrow.'

Blaine heard the click as she replaced the receiver.

He thumbed quickly through the Pascua

telephone directory for Sivo's home number, dialled and waited as the ring tone sounded in his ear. Then he heard Ethel Sivo's voice.

'Sivo residence. Ethel Sivo speaking.'

'Ethel, this is Blaine Carter. Is Joe there?'

'He went out at about half past eight.'

'Can I get in touch with him?'

'I can get a message to headquarters. They will relay it to him if he is in his car. If not they will keep trying.'

'I'm at home.'

'I'll do it right away. And Blaine. My sympathy to you and Amy.'

'Thank you.' He replaced the receiver and sat back in his chair and waited.

It took only seven minutes for Sivo to call.

'Blaine?'

'Joe. About those photographs.'

'What about them?' Sivo's voice reflected his displeasure.

'You can have them. Every single one.' He paused for a moment. 'You won't like what you see, but I believe they will help your investigation.'

'I'm certain they will. I'll send a man up immediately.'

'I'll be waiting.' Still holding the receiver he pressed and released the cradle switch. He began to dial Wendy Borland's number.

*   *   *

In the telephone box at Bougainville, Mack replaced the receiver and pushed the door open.

'Olaf Greeb wasn't happy. When I told him I could not contact Carter, he agreed to meet us at the marina.'

He shut the telephone directory. 'I'll try him once more.'

Emma paced away from the telephone box and leaned against the car. A light breeze was picking up and in the silence she heard Mack dialling. She looked across the water where the moon, still low in the sky, cast a bright silver ribbon from the horizon to the shore.

Mack pushed the door open. 'No good. His phone is still engaged. We'll have to go without him.'

As they drove off, the man who had followed them came out from an alley just behind the telephone box. He dialled and listened to the ring-tone. A voice answered.

'Yes?'

'This is Grant. I'm at Bougainville. They called on Bruneau.'

'Have they found her?'

'She wasn't with them when they left. I'm convinced the Bruneaus took her somewhere.' He paused. 'I've found the car. It's in Bruneau's garage. Her suitcase was on the back seat. I've got it in my car.'

James Riley took a long breath. 'Are the papers in the case?'

'No. And nothing in the car.'

'Damn.' He thought for a moment. 'Where are those two now?'

'On the way to Crab Island. They think she's there. I heard him calling Carter's skipper.'

'Go after them.'

'Now? In the dark?'

'Use my boat again. I'll phone my skipper now. He'll be waiting on the *Dandy Girl* when you get there. And Grant.'

'Yes?'

'This time search the bloody attic.'

*   *   *

Victor Bellamy's photographic studio was located in a grubby street off Sugar Terminal Drive. It was crammed between the walls of two double-storey buildings that were once the comfortable homes of well-to-do businessmen whose fortunes were founded on a fledgeling fishing industry. In those days the island had not yet seen the rapid development into a desirable Pacific tourist destination. It was hard to believe that the small village that existed here then was the incipient Pascua City of tall buildings and wealthy tourists.

Constable Forrest stopped the car in front of the studio. The ground floor was in darkness, but a light glowed behind the curtains of the living-quarters above the shop. Reeking rubbish-bins were lined up in front of several buildings whose dingy walls matched the dreary, decaying appearance of the whole area. Street lamps glowed dimly from rusted lampposts.

Williams hammered on the door. There was a long silence, then a window above them creaked open and a face peered down at them.

'Who are you?'

Williams said: 'Police. Open up.'

'What do you want?'

Williams said irritably: 'What we don't want is to stand here all night shouting up to an idiot looking out of a window. Get down here now.'

The head retreated, the window was closed and in a few minutes a light went on and they heard the sound of a key turning in the lock.

Victor Bellamy stood in the doorway and looked at the policemen in resentful silence. He was a thin man with black, wavy hair that hung to his shoulders. His face betrayed his alcoholic lifestyle, and his eyes were sunken and bloodshot. He was dressed in old jeans and plaid shirt.

Williams said pleasantly; 'Aren't you going to invite us in to your more than humble abode?'

'What do you want?'

'Didn't you hear me? We want to come in and we want you to invite us.'

Bellamy sneered. 'No warrant.'

Williams smiled. 'Not at the moment, but

Inspector Sivo will have one here in about ten minutes and if he finds that you've been difficult—well—you know what he's like.'

Bellamy shifted uneasily. 'Sivo? What does he want with me?'

'He wants you to invite us in so that everything is nice and legal. Then he wants to talk to you about some photographs.'

Bellamy stood aside for the policemen to enter. Williams looked at him without moving.

'Say the magic words.'

'Damn you. Come in.'

Williams turned to his junior. 'You heard that, Forrest. Mr Bellamy kindly invited us into his home.'

'Yes, sir.'

'Don't call me sir. I'm not an inspector. Yet.' He followed Bellamy into the studio.

Surprisingly, the ground-floor shop was neat, with shelves on the left wall and a counter running the length of the back wall. The bottom step of a staircase was visible through a door behind the counter. On the right were two filing-cabinets and a large iron safe. Faded Kodak and Agfa posters were pinned to the walls.

Bellamy sat on a stool in front of the counter.

'Now what?'

Williams ignored the question. While Forrest took up a position at the left of the door, he walked aimlessly about the studio examining the merchandise on the shelves and the stock behind the counter. Eventually he drifted to the large safe. Without looking at Bellamy he said casually: 'I take it this is where you keep the dirty pictures.'

Bellamy stood up angrily. 'Here! I don't deal in that stuff. I run a respectable business.'

Williams looked at him coldly. 'Sit down, shut up, and wait for the inspector to come and we'll see what's in the safe and filing-cabinets. In the meantime I'll look around upstairs.'

'You can't do that. It's private.'

Williams looked pained. 'You wouldn't deprive your guests of a visit to your bathroom, would you?' He turned to Forrest. 'If he moves, settle him with a karate swing.'

He went up the stairs, not with any expectation of finding anything significant, but because the inspector would expect it. At the top of the stairs, a door on the left led to the bathroom and opposite that was a small kitchen. The bedroom was at the end of the passage ahead of him. Once more he was surprised to find that the living-rooms, though untidy, were clean; probably a daily maid, Williams thought. He made a cursory search of all the obvious hiding places, but the only nude picture was on a Pirelli calendar in the bedroom. He went downstairs.

Bellamy looked at him sullenly. 'Been enjoying the naughty picture?' Williams ignored him.

They waited in silence, with Bellamy pacing uncomfortably around the studio. He went upstairs three times and returned more morose than ever. While Forrest's stolid figure blocked the doorway, Sergeant Williams, at ease on the customer's stool at the counter, turned the pages of a photographic magazine, apparently unperturbed by Bellamy's discomfiture. The silence was broken only by a car passing in the street outside and the sound of small rodents in the eaves. He put the magazine on the rack as he heard a car draw up in the street outside.

When Sivo entered he was obviously irritable, a mood that Williams suspected was occasioned by his interview with the judge. Vicente was seldom pleased with Sivo's after-hours visits.

'Any problems?'

Williams shook his head. 'None. I had a look around upstairs, but I think everything is stashed in that safe.'

'Invited you in, did he?' Williams nodded.

The inspector produced a legal document from his inside pocket. He presented it to Bellamy.

'Mr Bellamy, this is a search warrant properly executed before Judge Vicente, a judge of the Pascua High Court and . . .'

'I know all about bloody search warrants. Get on with it. What are you looking for?'

Sivo nodded. 'Vice been here a couple of times, have they? Is that how you know about search warrants?' He gestured to the safe. 'Let's do it the easy way. I want all the prints and negatives of photos you took at Crab Island.'

Bellamy grinned happily. 'I've never been to Crab Island, much less taken photographs there.'

The inspector looked nonplussed. 'Then how did your logo get on a photograph taken at Crab Island?'

'Lots of people bring me rolls to develop. How am I to guess where they were taken?'

Williams watched Sivo's face and saw the signs of growing anger. Here it comes, he thought. Sivo walked towards the photographer who took a pace back as though he expected Sivo to strike him.

The inspector said quietly: 'Don't play silly buggers with me, Bellamy. Whether you took the photographs or merely developed them, you know which ones I want. If you don't produce them in one minute, I'm taking you in, charging you with obstructing a murder investigation, and while you're locked up I'll turn this place over so thoroughly you won't recognize it when you get out.' He walked to the safe. 'Is that clear enough for you?'

Bellamy's face reflected his shock.

'I don't know anything about a murder.' He knelt in front of the safe. 'You can have all the negatives in here.'

The inspector was incredulous. 'Juliet Carter's murder has been all over the papers. Crab Island belongs to the Carters, and you never knew about a murder.' He stood over the photographer. 'Any more damned procrastination, and I'll throw the book at you.'

Bellamy was subdued. The policemen could almost smell his fear.

'I'm sorry Mr Sivo. You can have everything I've got.' He swung open the safe door and handed a box of negatives to the inspector. 'This is everything I have from Crab Island.'

'Just be sure it is everything. I am in possession of some prints, and if the negatives of those prints are not here, I'll have you inside so fast it will make your head spin.'

Bellamy said sullenly. 'Every neg from Crab Island is in there.'

Sivo handed the box to Forrest. 'Take these to the car.' He turned to Bellamy. 'Who gave you the roll to develop?'

'Baldwins.'

'The courier service?'

'Yes.' He paused. 'And it's no good asking them. I tried that. Ronnie Baldwin said they were delivered by some lads. A different one every time.'

'Who called for them?'

'No one. I was instructed to send the prints to a Sydney address. A different one each time. Probably accommodation addresses.' He hesitated. 'I was told to hang on to the negs until further notice. No one ever asked for them.'

'Did you print any extras? You know. To improve your financial situation?'

Bellamy shook his head vigorously. 'Hell no. A voice on the telephone said that if I tried that I would end up like the body that washed up on Garden Beach at Pascua Petit. I believed him.'

'When was this?'

'Eighteen months ago.'

'How were you paid?'

'An envelope was dropped through the letter-box late at night.'

'How did they know how much the bill was?'

'They didn't. It was always about three times what it was worth.'

'And you never suspected a crime was being committed? You never thought of coming to us?' Sivo's voice reflected his disbelief.

Bellamy shrugged. 'What crime? It isn't illegal to develop nude photographs.'

Sivo grunted at this inescapable logic. 'Now be careful how you answer this. Have you any idea who may be behind this? Any inkling at all? I'm not asking for a sworn statement. Just a guess; even a remote one.'

Bellamy shook his head. 'None, Mr Sivo. I swear.'

'Not a word of this to anyone. Is that

understood? And if you learn anything useful be sure to get in touch with me at once.'

Williams went out to join Forrest in the car. Sivo drove his own car. As they drove off, Forrest said: 'Sergeant.'

'What is it?'

'What's a karate swing?'

'I haven't the faintest idea. It just sounded right at the time.'

Sivo drove directly to the underground parking at the Justice Building. At the entrance he waited for the other car to stop behind him. He called Forrest over. 'Take off, lad. Report to me tomorrow morning.'

'Yes sir. Thank you sir.'

In his office Sivo took off his coat and scowled at his loaded IN tray. Williams sighed. He knew what was coming. The inspector gestured to the pile of papers.

'Go through that lot and see if there is anything we need urgently. I'm going to wash up.' He went through to the bathroom.

When he returned Williams had cleared Sivo's desk and laid out three documents and a bulky envelope. This he handed to his superior.

'Photographs,' he said laconically. 'With a note from Carter. He says this is everything.'

Sivo nodded with satisfaction. 'Good.' He opened the packet and flicked rapidly through the prints. Then he read the note from Carter. He closed the packet and stowed it in the bottom drawer of his desk.

He said: 'And the other stuff?'

Williams gestured to the documents. 'The autopsy on Juliet Carter, and as far as the rest are concerned, it seems they've pre-empted us.'

The inspector raised his eyebrows. 'Pre-empt? Pre-empt? Where did you find a posh word like that?'

Williams said airily: 'I had a good education.'

Sivo grunted. 'Did you indeed? Well, who has pre-empted us and how?'

'Forensics. They have identified the tyre-cast. A task team went out with your list of suspects and has catalogued possible cars with those tyres. They added a few from carparks that were picked up by traffic police, Hastings at forensics has provided a preliminary fingerprint report of the ones lifted from Mrs Carter's bedroom.' He pushed over one of the documents. 'The task-team list isn't complete. They're still looking.'

Sivo's raised eyebrows reflected his astonishment.

'They've moved their backsides for a change. The Prime Minister must have put a bomb under the Commissioner.'

He looked up at Williams. 'Have you looked at the fingerprint report?'

Williams grinned. 'You were spot on. Five sets.'

'No balloon. There should have been a set of unidentifiable prints of someone wearing gloves.'

Williams's brow furrowed with puzzlement. 'Nothing like that in the report, sir.'

'Are you sure?'

'Certain. I read it through carefully.'

'Hmm. And this is the list of people with Michelin tyres.' It was a short list of ten names. Two of them were people he knew. Williams saw the wolfish smile. Sivo underlined one of the names and handed the paper to Williams.

'Leave a message for a constable to locate that car and see if the wheels still have Michelins tomorrow morning. If not, find the tyres that have been removed and send them to forensics. They know what to look for if it's found. And Sergeant.'

'Yes sir.'

'As quietly as possible. I don't want the owner alerted. In any case he could be an innocent citizen.'

'What about the others?'

Sivo shook his head. 'Eight hired cars and someone who could never be involved.'

'How can you be sure?'

Sivo said irritably: 'Some idiot has included the Prime Minister's private car.' Williams hid a smile. Sivo continued. 'What about the autopsy?'

'Apart from the confirmation of the medical examiner's preliminary opinion of manual strangulation, there was one interesting aspect. Juliet Carter was loaded with a barbiturate. Probably self-administered.'

'That's why the bedclothes showed no sign of a violent struggle, no matter how vicious the strangulation might have been.' Sivo looked thoughtful. 'Her attacker did not like her very much. What puzzles me is why she said she wanted to talk to Carter when he came home and then took a sleeping tablet.'

Williams shrugged. 'Is it material?'

The inspector shook his head. 'Not necessarily. She was a regular user to judge by the bottles in the bathroom cabinet. She probably knew how much to take to get enough sleep until he came home.' He took the autopsy report from Williams and glanced at it briefly.

'Do you want to look through the photographs?'

Sivo yawned. 'Not now. I'll leave that until morning. If they contain—or don't contain—certain items, I want to be nice and fresh when I go and arrest the killer with a motive as old as time.'

'Oh?'

'Yes, Williams. Even a biblical king was aware of it.'

Williams looked at him with astonishment, but knowing how stubbornly reticent the inspector could be, wisely decided not to comment.

The inspector stood up.

'Ring Carter and remind him that his wife's room must remain sealed and locked until I release it. The police tape across the door must remain intact.' He tapped the autopsy report on his desk. 'Tell him forensics will release Juliet Carter's body in three days.' He put on his coat. 'Oh, and Williams.'

'Yes, sir.'

'You can run along and propose to that girl of yours now.'

Williams sighed with exasperation as Sivo went out of the office. Sometimes the inspector's jokes could get really tiresome. Before he could pick up the telephone it rang. He saw the inspector put his head back in the doorway. He waited for Williams to answer it.

The sergeant put the handset to his ear.

'Inspector Sivo's office.' He listened, then covered the mouthpiece. 'It's Uva Point. They have a signal from a boat off Crab Island. The *Amyrillis*. It sounds urgent.'

CHAPTER FIFTEEN

As Mack guided the Mercedes through the moonlit countryside, Emma remained silent and tense as she pondered the plight of the girl who had been abandoned on Crab Island. The friend that she remembered was high-spirited

195

and fun-loving with a sunny disposition and laughter that reflected her joy at just being alive. However, for the last year, her infrequent letters had betrayed a disquiet over some secret concerns that had affected her disposition to the extent that her normal ebullience was absent. Through the letters, Emma slowly came to understand the scope of Amy's distress.

It was not just the latest, almost hysterical, communication that had led Emma to her decision to come to Pascua. It was the gathering indications of some unnamed fear that had finally convinced Emma that her friend needed her. Not that she believed it was only through her intervention that Amy's difficulties, whatever they were, could be resolved. Indeed, she was honest enough to admit to herself that her presence could be no more than a salve to her friend's emotional wounds. It was this conviction that had brought her to a decision to defy all her family's sensible logic. Now she felt vindicated, and was satisfied that logic had no place alongside an instinctive desire to be with a friend in need.

The car headlights bored into a dank diaphanous mist that was rising over the moonlit countryside. On the road ahead the mist swirled as it escaped on either side of the speeding car.

Mack glanced at Emma, whose tightly

clasped fingers in her lap betrayed her deep concern for her friend. For a brief moment he wished they had not come on this uncertain endeavour. His only concern was for Emma. He had promised Teig that he would see she came to no harm, a promise that was becoming increasingly precarious.

There was no doubt in his mind that there were dangerous people involved in this affair. During his extensive and successful period in the private inquiry business he had learned that villains followed a subject for only two reasons: to harm the quarry or to learn what he knows. Hitherto it appeared that their follower merely wanted to learn what he thought they would discover, but the situation could change dramatically if they were successful in their quest. It was then that they would be at the greatest risk.

They left the cane lands and began the long climb that skirted the mountain. The sea on the left was silver, with a great pool of moonlit water meeting the sky at the horizon. In an hour the moon would be almost overhead. They should be arriving at Crab Island just then. He took no pleasure in the prospect of visiting that strange place of strange creatures. He knew that Emma dreaded the idea, but he knew too that she had more courage than many men with whom he had shared danger in the past.

As they left the mountain behind them they

descended the long stretch of road that took them to the city. He glanced briefly at the girl beside him. The signs of exhaustion were there in the drawn mouth and slumped shoulders. For a moment he wished he could leave her with Carter, but in her determination to find Amy, she would resist any attempt to leave her behind. Although she was not a blood-relative, he loved her as dearly as he would have loved his own child had he been fortunate enough to have one. She was everything a daughter should be and it was not surprising that she was cherished by Teig and her grandfather.

When he first saw her, she was a little girl of eight, and even then he knew she was someone special. Although he was only a surrogate father, she had always given him the respect and love she would have given her own father. Though he professed to be exasperated by her teasing references to 'Daddy Dear', he was secretly delighted at being elevated to that relationship.

He took the detour that skirted the city, and soon they were parked at the small-boat basin. Olaf was waiting, and ready to cast off.

*   *   *

When Amy left the château that morning, she had no inkling of the terror that would befall her before nightfall.

The day began inauspiciously with her

198

decision to hide on Crab Island being vehemently opposed by Françoise and Howard Bruneau. She had slept very little, her overheated imagination equating every sound with the demons that she believed were bent on destroying her. She was steadfast in her refusal to speak of the man of whom she was so afraid. All their attempts to persuade her to stay at La Brède were of no avail. Amy was distraught and frightened, threatening to go off on her own if they refused to help her.

Finally Françoise, who was flying to Sydney that day on a short holiday, agreed to take her to Crab Island. It would mean leaving her alone on the island if Françoise was to return to Pascua in time for her flight. This was not as callous as it would seem. There were times when both girls, still young teenagers, had spent solitary days on the island. Amy had always been the independent one during those blissful years, and Françoise had no doubts about Amy's ability to fend for herself. She shared none of Amy's belief in some sinister individual bent on harming her. After all, Crab Island was as much her home as Hungry Mountain was.

The sun was already warm on their faces when they met the swells on the calm, open sea. There was only the occasional splash of a leaping fish to disturb the smooth water. The air was clean and crisp with a light air coming in from the east. Their craft, a small open fishing-boat powered by a twenty-horsepower Johnson, crossed the channel in about twenty minutes.

In the distance they saw a cabin cruiser swinging wide on the south end of Crab Island as it sped towards Pascua. It passed about a mile on their port bow. Françoise watched it disappear behind them, her brow furrowed with puzzlement. What, she thought, was the Riley boat doing out so early? She looked at Amy who was concentrating her gaze on the island. She did not appear to have noticed the cruiser which was now out of sight.

Françoise, with one of her father's overalls covering her good travelling outfit, now concentrated on steering deftly through the channels until the boat nudged the sandy beach. Both women sat for a moment savouring the sounds of the sea lapping softly against the shore.

'Remember?' asked Françoise, as she stepped from the prow on to the dry sand.

Amy smiled wanly. 'A long time ago.'

'My parents and your father. We all came here together. Our two families. Those whole blissful weekends we spent here.' Françoise shook her head slowly. 'And then we didn't come any more. What happened?'

Amy said fiercely. 'Juliet came.' The bitterness was thick, her voice harsh. Then the tears flowed. 'Oh Fran. Why did he marry her?' She sobbed uncontrollably.

Fran drew her gently from the boat and held her. When the sobs had subsided, she hoisted the food basket from the boat and carried it up the beach. Amy followed with the tog bag she had brought with her. She set it down and unzipped it. She took out a slim folder, checked the contents and slid it back into the bag.

Fran looked at her curiously. 'Why are you hanging on to that?'

'It has something to do with Juliet's murder. I don't know how yet, but I know I must keep this for the police.'

'I still think you should have gone straight to the police if you have anything that will help them.'

'No. No, no. I don't know who to trust.'

Fran detected a tone of rising hysteria. She held the girl briefly. 'Hush. You're safe here. Hush.' She realized that Amy was still being driven by irrational fears. Her doubts about leaving the girl here returned but she shrugged them off. Anyway it was too late now. She had to be in Sydney by tomorrow morning. Amy had always been strong and resilient. She would be safe here, Fran thought. She isn't in any real danger. Amy was merely reacting to the horrifying circumstance of Juliet's murder.

Fran's father had attempted to question her, to glean whatever he could of whom or what she feared, but she only became hysterical. He had left it then and decided that she only needed time. Time to come to her senses and realize that her fears were unfounded and merely the product of her terrifying experience.

Fran led the way along the path to the house. She went through to the kitchen with Amy following meekly behind her. Together they stowed the few provisions in the store cupboard and her bags on the top shelf. Fran locked the cupboard and handed Amy the key. There were no perishables so they decided not to switch on the refrigerator. Together they went into the main bedroom.

Fran lifted the bag on to the bed and regarded Amy dubiously.

'Are you sure you want to do this?'

Amy nodded. 'I'm certain. You'd better go.'

Fran hugged her briefly and left the house. Amy followed her to the beach and watched her friend steer the boat slowly through the reefs to open water. Amy had a brief moment of doubt and apprehension, then her resolve hardened and she walked on to the small jetty and sat with her legs dangling in the water, oblivious of her sodden sneakers. She watched for a long time as the boat grew smaller and disappeared into the brightening morning haze.

She decided she would not go into the house immediately, but walk along the beach, going right around the island until she came back to her point of departure. She had done this many times in her childhood. She knew it would take her about half an hour; not hurrying, but savouring the sights and sounds of the island; the muted rumble of the surf out on the reef, the swish of the incoming waves on the beach, the cries of the seabirds, and the sight of the giant crabs scuttling for the safety of the bush as they spied her approach.

She enjoyed the company of the crabs. As a child she recognized regular visitors to the coconut groves and a friendly fisherman from Lea Buka, a village on the north-west coast of Pascua, taught her how to pick them up and how to pull them from their burrows with safety.

Her spirits began to lift as she walked. The enjoyment she used to feel at exploring the island as a child slowly returned as she came upon long-forgotten landmarks. She felt the softness of the sand under the soles of her sneakers; then, where the tumble of rocks spread from the bush into the deep water, she felt the sun's warmth on her hands and feet as she scrambled across to continue her walk on the other side. She stopped and inspected rock pools where tiny sea creatures had been trapped as the tide receded.

She had read once that the English painter Christopher Wood had described his first years in Paris as *wind in the face freedom*. She always remembered and cherished that as an apt description of her days on Crab Island.

She had always felt safe on the island. It was a refuge that she had shared with her father, but it was a measure of the shock and horror of the previous night's events that she never once considered letting him know where she was. Perhaps an analyst would have suggested that her growing disenchantment with her father's ability to protect her from her stepmother, combined with the row with Juliet and the unsatisfactory interview with Blaine, created in her mind a determination to isolate herself. Added to this was the fear that his knowledge of her whereabouts might unwittingly be communicated to the person she feared.

As she rounded the northern headland and continued along the eastern shore, she recalled how awed she had always been by the vista of limitless ocean from this side of the island. On clear days however, Pascua Grande could be seen from the opposite, western, shore as a dark smudge on the horizon, and that—quite irrationally—appeared to her to place limits on the vastness of the sea in that direction. It was a vestigial perception from her childhood, but it remained in her subconscious.

It was during her childhood too that she first learned that the islanders captured their favourite delicacy, the giant octopus, by diving down in pairs to the submarine caves where the beasts lived. She often saw them emerging from the shallow water carrying their catch to the boats just off-shore.

She was still on the beach approaching the path to the house, and screened by a small bush, when all at once she heard a distant buzzing sound which she recognized immediately as the noise of a marine engine. From the southern tip of the island a small open boat appeared. As it raced towards her, she froze in terror, her recently acquired contentment swept away and fear sent her sobbing and stumbling into the bushes. She missed the path and ran blindly into dense thicket, the thorns clutching and tearing at her like the hands of the monster who had killed her stepmother. She fell into the edge of an impenetrable underbrush and lay there, knees drawn up, stifling the sobs which she was sure could be heard across the island. Her few minutes of fragile coherence drowned in a return of the horror and fear that had engulfed her the previous night.

The buzzing grew closer until it seemed to be all around her. Then it stopped suddenly and she heard the hiss of the boat's wake as it swept across the sand.

There was a long silence.

Then from the depths of her fear, a long-forgotten instinct for self-preservation clawed its way into her consciousness.

She moved so that she was kneeling, her head level with a screen of branches and leaves. She was certain the visitor had not seen her, yet her terror remained. The boat had stopped right opposite the path and was being turned so that the prow faced the channel. It was almost as though the boat was being positioned for a fast retreat.

The visitor wore a woollen balaclava and dark glasses, with a scarf around the mouth. Amy was completely still. The sobs had subsided and she breathed slowly and silently. The stranger stood looking around, wary and suspicious. There was a long silence as each of them watched, the one unaware of the presence of the other. Amy knew instinctively that this was danger, and even without her recent harrowing encounter, she knew she would have been afraid of this invasion of her personal paradise.

She remained still. The sounds which had been excluded from her consciousness by the violence of her fear, began to return. The surf still pounded in the distance and the sea birds called across the water. The menace began to take on a form that she could dimly comprehend.

At last the intruder appeared to be satisfied and walked swiftly along the path to the house. Amy listened to the sound of soft footsteps on the leafy path and waited until there was silence. She wasn't sure who the stranger was, but she thought she knew why her stepmother had been murdered, and she was in possession of the same information. This made her equally vulnerable.

She pushed aside the boughs of the shrub that hindered her path out of the woods and ran swiftly along the shore towards the southern headland. Near the point at which the newcomer had appeared was a narrow path to the engine room which housed the source of their power. It was a small concrete structure with a slate roof that stood in a clearing a hundred and fifty metres from the house. She was glad now that she had not switched on the refrigerator, for the thudding of the engine would have alerted the prowler to her presence. The shrubbery had closed in to within a few feet of the building, but the side facing the house had been cleared recently. She opened the door. At once she was assailed by a long-remembered smell of oil, damp leaves and rotting vegetation. She stood panting and taking great gasps of air.

The diesel-engine and generator combination stood on its plinth in the centre of the room, occupying most of the floor space. There was a small locked cupboard in the corner which she knew contained tools for the maintenance of the plant. The motor and generator were wiped over and spotlessly clean, testimony to the efficiency of the maintenance electrician who came over once a month to service the equipment. This evidence of normality caused Amy to pause just inside the doorway for a moment to take stock of the danger facing her. Her fears subsided a little as she remembered that her advantage lay in her extensive knowledge of the terrain; she knew every hidden approach to the house and every useful place of concealment.

Just above the height of her head, ventilation gaps had been left in the concrete wall. When she stood on the plinth her eyes were level with the gaps. She looked across the lawn at the main building. There was no one in sight, and while she had to assume the visitor had gone into the house, she still felt uneasy. The garden was deserted and silent, with the merest hint of a breeze twitching the leaves in the taller trees. Amy waited.

While she had no idea of the identity of the intruder, she did not rule out the possibility that it was the person who had killed Juliet. The approach around the eastern shore and the reluctance to use the jetty indicated a desire for anonymity. The surreptitious approach to the house was significant and equally suspicious. She had been wise to remain unseen. She continued to wait.

All at once her heart pounded and she froze with terror as she heard a rustle of leaves outside the door behind her. Then came the sound of soft scraping. She stood for a long moment, listening to the silence. Then the sound came again and she forced herself to move. She bent low and crept silently around the generator until she was opposite the door. Then the sound came once more. She raised her head and peered into the bush from the corner of a ventilator. Nothing. The scraping sound came once more, this time from below the ventilator. Then she knew. She moved silently to the door and flung it open.

'Bloody crabs!'

Outside, a family of enormous coconut-crabs scuttled into the bush and hid themselves in the undergrowth. Heart pounding with relief and anger, she went back to her perch at the vent. Then hallucination slid slyly into her fragile senses and for a brief moment she saw an image of a crab metamorphosing into a human with balaclava and dark glasses. Then the image disappeared and rationality returned.

Slowly, as she stood motionless on the plinth, staring at the house, she heard the deep, faraway sound of an approaching vessel. Keeping the machine room between her and the house, she went out of the door and listened. There was no mistake. Another craft, a bigger one, was cruising to the west of the island. Until she heard the note of the engine drop to idling speed, and the unmistakable rise and fall as it negotiated the narrow channel through the reef, she was not sure it was making for Crab Island.

Panicky now she went quickly back to her perch on the plinth and looked through the ventilator. She saw the stranger run from the house with a handful of white paper or

209

cardboard. Photographs? Then the stranger fell, scattering white cards on the path. Hurriedly they were gathered up, but Amy did not wait to see what followed. She retreated into the undergrowth and hid deep in the woods. She was convinced that the newcomers were part of the conspiracy, and had come to find her and the document she had hidden in her bag in the store cupboard.

When she finally stopped, dishevelled, exhausted and afraid, she knew she was safe for the moment.

She had barely hidden herself when, from the eastern shore, she heard a motor roar into life. She heard men shouting and the diminishing buzz of the first intruder's boat as it rounded the southern headland.

Then there was silence.

Amy lay back behind a screen of thick undergrowth and waited. She was chagrined at the thought that her refuge had proved to be a more dangerous place than she had first supposed. She would have been safer at the home of the Bruneaus where at least she would have had support and protection. For the first time she realized that her precipitous flight from the house at Bougainville had been hasty and foolish, as was her desire to hide in these bushes. She decided that, caught unawares, she was running about without any idea of what the danger was or from whom it would come.

She decided she needed a plan. She pondered for a moment and then decided that there were three elements to her strategy. She needed to know who the intruders were, what they were doing and when they would leave. All this could only be achieved by observation. Skulking in the bushes would not achieve her objectives. She realized that all this was simple and obvious, but it was a start and her resolve gave her the courage to face her fears. She had always been self-reliant, and she recognized for the first time how much the awful events had diminished her self confidence. She moved cautiously into the open and went back to her look-out in the power room. As she opened the door, she heard the loud click of the relay switch which activated the motor when a light was turned on in the house. The motor started up, startling her for a moment, but it shut down again immediately. At once she guessed that whoever was in the house was a stranger, testing the unfamiliar fixtures. She guessed too that if they were strangers, they were unlikely to search the bushes. A stranger was unlikely to know that the crabs were completely harmless if they were left alone.

She took up her position at the ventilator and decided to wait them out.

It was half an hour before she heard the roar of the cruiser's engines starting up. She was able to track its cautious departure through the reef until the sound of its engines died away. She waited patiently in the power room, watching the house for any signs of life. Nothing stirred, and when she saw the crabs emerge from the undergrowth and approach the windfall coconuts on the lawn, she knew the house was empty. The crabs were the first to know.

She waited another ten minutes before she left the power room and took an oblique approach towards the house. She stood outside a window and listened carefully for sounds of occupation, but there were none. Still cautious and apprehensive she walked silently to the front door where she stood at the edge of the glass pane and listened.

Finally she opened the door and entered the house. She went from room to room, but the visitors had left no evidence of their presence. She opened the store-cupboard, looked distastefully at the provisions, saw nothing she liked and retrieved her tog bag. She went to the main bedroom, sat on the bed and considered her position. Her dysfunctional imagination saw enemies everywhere and in her irrational state she believed she had to organize a protective shield against intruders who entered the house while she slept.

It took her only twenty minutes to arrange her defences and her eyes glittered as she contemplated the effect on an intruder.

She showered and changed her clothes, then lay on the bed and slept.

CHAPTER SIXTEEN

Moonlight slanting across the calm water from the east washed the surface with a silvery-grey radiance. The air was warm and humid and as the *Amyrillis* raced through the water towards Crab Island a cloud of flying fish, alarmed by hungry predators, left the water ahead of them and floated for several seconds before returning to the deep.

Olaf turned his head. 'Bluefish running,' he said.

Mack looked across the bow. 'Bluefish?'

'Yah. When they come to the islands to spawn they hunt the flyers.' He changed course slightly. 'Storm coming.'

Emma sat up. 'A storm? But it's so calm.'

He pointed to the water ahead of them. 'Saint Elmo's fire.' They looked down to see a phosphorescent glow running at the tips of the bow-wave. He pointed towards the west. A long black line of clouds was just visible on the horizon. 'In about three hours.' As though to support his prediction, a gust of wind ripped across the water, sending a spray from the bow-wave on to the windscreen. It was followed by a muted roll of thunder. Emma looked back over the stern and saw distant flashes in the dark line of clouds.

Crab Island appeared ahead of them, a dark

mound that grew as they closed in on it.

Mack stood and peered through the windscreen. 'Can you see any lights?'

Olaf shook his head. 'You can't see lights from the sea. Too much bush.'

Before they reached the reef, Mack said: 'Stop the boat for a moment.' Olaf pushed the lever forward and the noise of the motors dropped to a low bubble. The prow dipped and the boat's momentum carried it on for about thirty metres. 'We don't want to announce our arrival.'

Emma was puzzled. 'You mean we sneak up on Amy? Why?'

'Because we don't know her state of mind. She may hide from us as she did this morning.'

'But she didn't know who we were then.'

'And she doesn't know who we are now.'

Emma thought for a moment. 'Of course. I'm tired. I'm not thinking straight.'

'We have to go in quietly.'

Olaf nodded his agreement. 'What about rubber dinghy?'

'Do you have one? On board?'

'Of course. Pascua Fisheries Board insist. Every cabin craft must carry one for safety.' He activated the anchor winch and switched off the motors. He went back to a port locker and took out a tightly wrapped bundle and a large air tank. He took them to the stern-well and connected the hoses. As Emma and Mack watched him, he inflated the dinghy. As it grew

214

to about three metres, he let it drop over the side and lashed a line to a cleat. The paddle was located in a stern locker. It was in two parts which he fitted together. When he had placed the paddle in the dinghy he took two flashlights from a drawer under the control panel. He switched them on and off to test them and handed one to each of them. 'I stay with boat. If you flash four times from the jetty I will bring the boat in.'

Emma stepped into the dinghy. 'You paddle. I've never been in one of these.'

'Aye aye, Captain.' He handed his torch to her to hold.

Olaf held his arm and pointed. 'Another boat.'

About half a mile away the dark shape of another cabin cruiser, running without lights, was moving swiftly around the north of Crab Island. The note of its engines could be heard clearly across the water. It kept well clear of the reefs and disappeared from sight. The note of the motors stopped abruptly.

Olaf was angry. 'That's the *Dandy Girl*. Stupid, stupid man, running without lights. He is a danger to others.' He turned to face Mack. 'And with no lights he tells us he is here for no good reason. Stupid.'

Mack's voice took on a note of urgency. 'You're right. They're up to mischief. We'd better get over there.' He paused. 'Who is the owner?'

'A man named Riley. Head of Tourist Board.'

Mack thought for a moment. He said: 'Give me some paper.' Olaf took a small pad from a drawer and handed it to him. Mack scribbled a long message and handed it to Olaf. 'Radio the Uva Point office and ask them to get that message to Sivo. This is more complicated than I thought. We'd better get him into this.' He stepped gingerly into the dinghy. 'Let's go, Emma.'

'What's in the note?'

Mack explained briefly. With Emma seated comfortably behind him, Mack paddled across the reef towards the jetty. They beached the dinghy near the mangroves and pushed it under a low bough. It wasn't completely hidden but it was unlikely that it would be seen in the dark shadow of the mangroves.

The breeze had lifted to a good blow. The dark trees rattled and swayed. Clouds began to drift overhead, but as yet there was no sign of the storm that Olaf had predicted.

Mack led the way along the path, hesitating now and then as they entered deep shadows. The noisy chorus of innumerable insects accompanied them as they walked quietly towards the dark, silent house.

Mack stopped at the edge of the coconut-grove and waited for Emma to come alongside him.

*   *   *

Sivo replaced the telephone and began removing his coat. Williams sighed.

'I gather we're not finished for the night.'

'No we're not,' Sivo snapped. 'The *Dandy Girl* is swarming around Crab Island without running lights.' He sat heavily in his chair. 'I know Riley has bums and bosoms for brains. Now I'm convinced he's demented as well.'

'Are you sure Riley is aboard?'

'I didn't say he's aboard,' the inspector said irritably. 'No he's not aboard. Uva Point said the skipper and Riley's man Grant are the only two out there. It seems the message originated with that McGlashan fellow.' Joe Sivo's face was creased with fatigue lines. Another minute, he thought morosely, and I could have been on my way home. Lightning flashed over the Bay followed by a long roll of thunder.

'What are we going to do about it?'

'Not a damn thing.' The inspector looked kindly at Williams. 'And thank you for the "we". You don't have to stay.'

'I'll stay as long as you do.'

'Captain Glasspoole at Uva wanted to bring them in and charge them, but checked with me first in case it's relevant to our murder case.'

'And is it?'

'No it isn't. McGlashan and that girl obviously think Amy Carter is on Crab Island. What they're doing out there doesn't interest

217

me.' He paused. 'Unless . . .' He paged quickly through the directory and dialled. The phone was answered almost immediately. 'Mrs Bruneau? This is Inspector Sivo. Is Amy Carter with you?' He listened for a moment. 'I see. Thank you, Mrs Bruneau.'

The sergeant watched him replace the receiver with a gentle hand and knew that Sivo was angry. 'Is Amy Carter on the island?'

'She is.' Sivo's anger was evident in the set of his jaw. He stood up and walked to the window. 'What a stupid lot the human race is.' His voice rasped with frustration. 'How the hell could they allow her to go to the island alone?'

'Alone?' Williams was incredulous.

Sivo nodded, turned from the window and sat at his desk. 'We'll see what Riley has to say.' He dialled and listened. He sat back when the phone was answered. 'Riley? Sivo. Yes I do know the bloody time so don't take that tone with me. No. You listen to me. What the hell is your boat doing at Crab Island?'

The inspector is really angry, Williams thought. I wouldn't be in Riley's shoes.

'You have every right to send your boat anywhere you damn please, but you will not send your boat out without running lights. Yes, that's right. No running lights. Your skipper has been ordered back to Uva Point where your boat will be impounded and he will be charged. Barry Glasspoole is as angry as I am.'

Sivo paused for a long time listening to the voice at the other end of the telephone. 'What was in those documents?' Another long pause. 'Then we'll get them from Amy Carter when we find her on Crab.' He slammed down the handset, stood up, walked to the window and took several deep breaths.

'Do you want me to go there?'

Sivo stood for a long time before he turned and said, 'Thank you, no.' He sat down once more, picked up the phone and dialled. When it was answered he said: 'Barry? Sivo. A favour. Please ask Olaf Greeb to keep me informed of all developments as they occur.' He listened for a moment. 'No, Barry. I won't go out there. Now or later. I'll be here for another hour.'

Williams smiled ruefully. 'I'm glad *I'm* not married.'

'If you're under the impression that Ethel will be irritated, you're wrong,' Sivo growled. 'She's used to this.'

Williams was all innocence. 'I didn't mean to suggest that . . .'

'I know what you didn't mean to suggest, so can it.' The inspector looked at him speculatively. 'Why Billy Williams?'

'What do you mean?'

'Billy is for William, is it not? Why did your parents name you William Williams?'

'They are devout Taffys.'

'What? Both of them?'

'Both of them.'

'Lord!' The inspector thought for a moment. 'Well, I suppose you won't be proposing to that nice lass tonight. May as well keep ourselves busy.' Sivo took Blaine Carter's packet of photographs and Bellamy's box of negatives from the bottom drawer of his desk and placed them squarely between Williams and himself. 'There are eight nudes amongst that lot.' He dumped the negatives on the desk. 'I want each nude matched to its negative. Let's begin.'

*   *   *

Mack moved a few steps along the edge of the shrubbery. The house was in darkness.

On the expanse of moonlit lawn at least six black shapes crawled slowly towards the coconut-grove, searching for the fruit that would sustain them in their burrows during the daylight hours. Emma shuddered. 'Those crabs give me the creeps.'

Mack pointed to an open window; it was the only one open on this side of the house. She oriented herself against her memory of the bedroom doors off the passage. Yes. It was the main bedroom.

Mack guessed that Amy was either sleeping or she had left the house to hide in the bushes. If she was asleep, that is where she would be. There was only one obvious choice; they had to search the house first.

'Stay close,' he whispered. 'We have to stay in the shadows, move to the side of the house and go to the front along the wall.'

Emma nodded, then realized he could not see her in the dark. 'You're the boss. Lead on.' She paused. 'I suppose shouting *Amy. It's Emma Delaney. I've come to take you home* is a bad idea.'

'A very bad idea. If she thinks it's a trick, she'll hide and we'll never find her.' He shook his head. 'No. We have to do it the hard way.'

'It was just a thought.'

With Mack leading the way they circled the house, all the while remaining in the shadows until they arrived at the front door. Mack took the handle and was about to turn it when suddenly there was a distant roar as a boat engine thundered into life.

'Damn. That's just what we don't need at this moment. Get down.' They crouched below the opaque lower half of the door. 'We'll have to wait until it's gone.'

Emma mouthed softly: 'What is that?'

'The *Dandy Girl*. The skipper must have got his marching orders. We'll wait and see if anything stirs.'

They waited in silence. There was no sound from the house. As the cruiser faded into the distance, the only sound was the distant thunder of the surf and the soft whine of the rising wind. The moonlight faded for a moment as a cloud drifted overhead. They heard the rumble of thunder a long way off. They continued to wait. The house remained silent.

Motioning to Emma to stay where she was, Mack stood upright and looked through the glass door into the living-room. It was silent and deserted with only the dark, crouching shapes of the furniture visible in the reflected moonlight. With a gentle hand he turned the door handle. The door opened on silent hinges. He signalled Emma to follow him.

The air in the house was warm, humid and stale. Emma's first impulse was to throw open all the windows as she did every morning at Cold Water Farm, but this was a house thousands of miles away from home. Their priority at this moment was Amy. The house was alive with small sounds, the wind in the eaves, the creak of roof beams contracting in the night air and the occasional rustling which sounded like rodents under the floor.

Mack touched her arm. He pointed to the passage on the left where the main bedroom was. Emma nodded and moved quietly through the arch. She heard a slight rustling sound and switched on her torch. She screamed as four pairs of malevolent red eyes stared at her.

Mack shouted: 'She's filled the passage with crabs.' There was the crash of a window being flung open. 'She's going through the window.'

He raced into the bedroom, dropping his torch as he went through the door. Emma watched him go, her limbs paralysed with shock. She heard him shout and then it was quiet. Finally she forced herself to move, making swiftly for the front door. Outside, she saw Mack in the middle of the lawn wrestling with Amy, trying to hold on to her as she fought insanely to free herself. Then from her throat came a thin screaming sound like a keen that echoed through the trees.

Emma ran to her, taking her arms as Mack held her. Amy was dishevelled and almost demented with terror. Emma knew that this was the worst possible way to deal with the terrified girl but there was no alternative.

'Amy. it's me, Emma.'

The girl continued to struggle. 'No. No. You're not Emma. Not Emma.' Then she sobbed uncontrollably. 'Please. Please. Don't hurt me.'

Emma held her arms, tears for her friend coursing down her cheeks. 'Amy. Amy. Listen to me. I'm Emma. Your Emma. From Cold Water Farm. I came to help you when you wrote to me.'

Slowly the struggles stopped, the sobbing slowed and she looked wide-eyed into Emma's face. When she spoke her voice was hoarse.

'Emma. My Emma.'

'Yes. It's me. Emma.'

Amy turned her face to Mack and abruptly

her knees folded, her eyes rolled back and she collapsed. Mack lifted her and carried her to the house, placing her gently on the bed in the main bedroom. Emma went ahead of him, turning on the lights and looking around nervously for the crabs. They were nowhere in sight. Then she heard them scuttling as they sought the freedom of the open front door.

Emma leaned over the bed and felt the girl's pulse. 'We can't move her until she recovers.' Emma stroked the hair away from Amy's face.

Mack went to the door. 'I'd better get Olaf to bring the boat to the jetty.' He paused. 'And ask Sivo to let Carter know we have his daughter.'

Emma nodded without looking up. 'Before you go out, bring me a jug of water and a glass.'

Mack went through to the kitchen.

As she moved Amy into a more comfortable position, Emma noticed a large manila envelope in the corner of the room. Emma picked it up and turned it over looking for an address. There was none, but in the corner was a small scribble. *Urgent—open immediately.* The gummed flap had been torn open.

Thoughtfully she tapped the edge of the envelope on her hand. She glanced at Amy who showed no sign of coming round.

Mack entered with the water. 'What's that?' He placed the water on the bedside table.

'I don't know. I found it on the floor. It was

open.' She frowned. 'Should we look inside?'

'Of course.' He took it from her. 'I know how squeamish you are about other people's privacy, but I used to be a tacky private eye, remember. I have no such scruples.' He drew out two photographs and a short letter. The subjects in the photographs were nude. He whistled and held up one of them for her to see. 'Recognize hers?'

'It's that stunning beauty we saw at the airport. No wonder she was bleating about getting the negatives.'

Mack pushed the prints back into the envelope. 'Sivo will love this.' He looked at the letter. It read:

Herewith the prints you ordered. Please remit payment to the address provided in our last note to you. The negatives will be sent on receipt of payment.

There was neither signature nor return address.

Mack looked down at the sleeping girl. 'I don't like her colour. I think we should get her to a doctor immediately.'

Emma nodded. 'I'll watch her while you bring Olaf in to the jetty.'

Mack picked up the flashlight and left the house.

*   *   *

Inspector Sivo looked along the row of photographs, each with a negative on top. There were two negatives on the table without prints.

'So what we have here are prints of eight nude bodies, and negatives of ten nude bodies.'

Williams was frowning as he examined a negative against the light. 'This one puzzles me, Inspector. Nine have identical backgrounds with the same portion of a picture behind the bed. This one looks as though it was taken in some dump. Iron bedstead and wash-basin.' He handed it to Sivo. 'Definitely not Crab Island furniture.'

Sivo peered at it. 'Hmm. Odd.' He looked thoughtful. 'I think we have something. Get Bellamy in first thing in the morning. Get our photo lab to print that. I think I know now where all this began.' He picked out two of the prints. 'We know who these people are. I want you to find out where they are now.' He scribbled on his pad. 'Go to immigration on the second floor and ask them for copies of these passport photos. Don't forget to take an indent form with our letterhead. Immigration are strict about these things.' He paused. 'And mention the Prime Minister a couple of times.'

Williams opened his notebook and ticked off the items. 'Call at photo lab. Passport photos. Check with tyres task team.' He looked up. 'You want the whole Carter ménage fingerprints taken for elimination?'

Sivo looked at him in astonishment. 'Ménage? Where the hell did that come from.'

'I told you . . .'

'I know. You had a good education. Yes. I want the whole household checked. There are six people at Hungry Mountain if you include the Martins and exclude the grooms.' He hesitated. 'The Martins are not Pascuan nationals so their prints will be filed in immigration with their residence permits.'

'Sir, I think there were seven.'

Sivo stood up and stretched. 'Of course. I forgot Sylvia Phillips.' He walked to the window and looked across the bay. High clouds were scudding across a closed-in sky. The sea was dark now, ominous with the threatening storm. 'Sylvia Phillips?' He went back to the desk. 'No. I think we can safely ignore her.' He sat. 'She's not a killer. She's a victim.'

Strange man, thought Wiliams. But as smart as they come. Aloud he said: 'What's the legal position?'

'We can't compel them.' He smiled and added blandly: 'But why would anyone refuse to be fingerprinted?'

The shrill ringing of the telephone startled them both. The inspector snatched up the receiver. 'Sivo.'

'Joe, this is Barry Glasspoole. We've had a message from Crab Island. McGlashan has found Amy Carter. They're on their way back here. They think the Carter girl may need medical attention.'

'I'll get on to it right away. And thanks, Barry.' Sivo pressed the cradle switch. 'Sergeant, get a paramedic team at the small-boat basin. They've found Amy Carter. I'll get on to Blaine Carter.'

As Williams picked up the other telephone, the inspector began to dial.

CHAPTER SEVENTEEN

Inspector Sivo was already removing his coat when he entered his office. To Williams this always signified prospects of a good day. The measure of the inspector's mood was the celerity with which he hung his coat on the hanger behind the door.

At the opposite end of the scale, any day when the inspector did not remove his coat at all was a day when his staff walked on tiptoes.

Today was going to be a good day. The inspector looked fresh, rested and ready for anything the city's felons could throw at him. In contrast to his wilted shirt and unshaven look of the night before, his pristine collar and smooth cheeks gave him the appearance of a man ready for battle. Williams sat opposite his superior and, pulling the OUT tray towards him, began his briefing. 'The photo lab sent the print down. It's still a little damp, but it's . . .' He slipped the photograph out of sight under a file as a petite, attractive young lady entered balancing a tray of coffee and a blue file.

'Good morning, Inspector.' She managed to deposit both on the desk without mishap.

Sivo took his coffee cup. 'Good morning, Sally. I hope you haven't come to propose.' Red-faced, Williams took his coffee to the window and stared out across the Bay. 'I'm afraid the sergeant is engaged at the moment; not matrimonially, I'm glad to say, but judicially.'

The girl smiled. 'Oh please, Inspector. You're embarrassing both of us.' She leaned on the desk, her hand displaying a diamond ring with ostentatious unconcern.

The inspector stared at it with disbelief. 'Good God. When did this happen? Williams, what *have* you done?'

The girl laughed out loud. Williams, recovering his composure, turned nonchalantly from the window. 'If you must know, it was yesterday when you went to the theatre to see Carter.'

Sally pouted. 'He said the only reason he finally proposed was because you told him to.'

'Nonsense,' Sivo growled. 'That was Mrs Sivo.'

'She told me she was advising you not to push him.'

'She told you that, did she?' The inspector shifted uncomfortably.

'At the same time she was advising me how to land him.'

Sivo looked at her with astonishment. 'Monstrous,' was all he could say.

'You see, sir, women *do* know best.' She giggled as she went out with the empty tray.

The inspector looked balefully at Sergeant Williams who kept a straight face.

'Stop smiling under your breath.' Then his voice softened. 'Congratulations.'

'Thank you, sir.' Williams went back to the desk. 'As I was saying, this is the print the lab sent over.'

'Put that aside for a moment. Is Bellamy here yet?'

'Yes sir. He's in the interrogation room.'

'How long has he been there?'

'About half an hour.'

'Good. Give him another half hour. He'll be busting to talk.'

'Have you heard from Mr Carter?'

'He's been at the hospital all night. He went home half an hour ago. The girl is still sedated, but the prognosis is very good. A psychiatrist is interviewing McGlashan and Mrs Olsen.' He took a file from the OUT tray. 'We will be told when she can make a statement.' He opened a file. 'Is this the final list of cars with Michelin tyres?'

'Yes sir. And they checked back. One car

had Michelin yesterday and Goodyear today. You were right again.'

'Indeed?' The inspector beamed. 'Things are looking up. We should have a villain in the slammer by tomorrow.'

Williams looked at him with surprise. 'Slammer, sir?'

The inspector nodded. 'I said slammer. Everyone else speaks American these days. Why can't I?'

'Indeed. Why not, sir. Shall I bring in Bellamy now?'

'Not just yet. I want a word with Carter.' He picked up the phone and dialled.

Mrs Garland answered. 'Carter residence.'

'Let me speak to Mr Carter please, Mrs Garland.'

'Yes, sir.' He heard the clatter of the receiver on the table, and again as it was picked up.

'Carter speaking.'

'Blaine. Joe Sivo. When is your current play closing?'

'Tonight. The theatre will be dark for a fortnight.' Sivo heard the strain in the voice. 'Why do you ask?'

There was a long pause. Sivo said quietly: 'I'm afraid I have to arrest four of your people in the next twenty-four hours.'

'Oh my God. Who are they?'

'I'll tell you who they are before I take them in.'

'Is one of them responsible for Juliet's death?'

'I can't answer that on the telephone. I'm sorry.'

There was a pause. 'I understand.'

Sivo rang off and looked up at the sergeant's startled gaze. He ignored it. 'Did the records office get contact numbers for those two I asked you to find?'

'Yes sir.' He took a file from the tray. 'Senator Morrison lives in New Jersey, and Mrs Reinholt lives in Perth.'

'I'll want to speak to both of them today.' He put the file aside. 'Both married?'

'Yes sir.'

'I see.' He scratched his chin, picked up the phone and dialled the Uva Point office. 'Barry? Sivo. Are you still holding those two Riley men? Good.' He listened for a short while. 'It's not a problem. I'll come down and charge them as soon as I've cleared my desk.' He frowned. 'On no account is Riley to see them. If he gets difficult refer him to me. Thanks, Barry.' He replaced the receiver. 'You can bring Bellamy in now, Sergeant.'

*   *   *

Blaine Carter drove out of the gates, his thoughts fixed on Sivo's devastating announcement.

Which four? And why?

232

He half-wished the inspector hadn't told him, but if it were inevitable he would be faced with the dilemma soon enough. All at once he became aware that his penchant for seeking procrastination was surfacing. He sighed. He could remember a time when he was decisive and determined, at times to the point of impetuosity. For years now he had refused to accept the facts of his marriage and his character had followed in the wake of growing vacillation, especially in matters of executive decision.

The morning was fresh and cool and behind him the mountain was framed by a clear blue sky. He drove with the windows down, a breeze caressing his face and his tired eyes. The night had been stressful, but Amy's rapid recovery buoyed his spirits and he felt almost cheerful.

The car-park at the theatre was empty as he drove in. His first emotion was one of disappointment which lasted for a fraction of a minute before he realized that he was at least an hour earlier than his normal time of arrival. His internal clock had been warped by his night at the hospital. He had slept for no more than a couple of hours and he resolved to leave early and sleep for at least three hours before returning for the evening performance. He would have to visit Amy too before then.

He made his customary inspection of the stage and auditorium, picked up a programme lying under an aisle seat, made a mental note to speak to the cleaners and sat in the second row to look at the set. The thought of this, the last performance of the play, triggered thoughts of his previous moments in this seat just over thirty-six hours ago. Since then, he had discovered more of his wife's infidelities, seen her strangled body, learned that his daughter had disappeared and then had been found, heard that four of his company were to be arrested and, most important, declared his love for Rhoda Larkin. Despite all this, or perhaps because of it, he smiled wryly. All his recent pain, and humiliation seemed irrelevant now. His father had encapsulated his attitude to misfortune in a few words: *It won't matter in fifty years.*

As he pondered his father's philosophy, he began to see the last two days in perspective. What the hell, he thought, I still have everything I had last week. Whatever fate could throw at him now would be a trifle compared with what he had gone through. At least he was alive. Then he remembered another of his father's utterances. *I have no fear of dying. I have a greater fear of living.*

Blaine pondered on the course his life had taken. By his own high standards he believed he was entitled to consider himself a man of integrity and while he knew there was no relationship between innocence and reward or crime and retribution, he sometimes felt that he had been short-changed by fate. He realized, of course, that if misfortune were the prize for evil and honesty were rewarded with good fortune, then children would never suffer the ravages of war, famine and disease. It was perhaps facile reasoning, but Blaine Carter was a sensitive yet uncomplicated man whose concepts of right and wrong were iron-clad.

Upstairs in his office he found an IN tray stacked with files. He removed his coat, opened the windows to catch the slight breeze and sat down at his desk. He looked at the tray with distaste. He wandered across to the window, wandered back to the bookcase and refused to admit that he was hoping Rhoda would knock at his door. He sighed and got down to work. He heard Wendy open her door and close it. His door opened. She looked at him inquiringly.

'Well?'

'Well what?'

'Don't be obtuse.' Her frown reflected her concern. 'How is Amy?' She regarded him critically for a moment. 'I hope she's better than you look. You look like hell.'

He nodded. 'Bingo. That's how I feel.' He pushed aside the files. 'Amy is improving. She was very lucky. She has two good friends who went the extra mile. I'm grateful to them.'

She sat down with a long sigh. 'She is a girl who will always have good friends. She deserves them.' She saw his eyes stray to the window as he heard cars arriving in the theatre car-park. 'What are you going to do about her?'

'About Amy?'

'You're being obtuse again. I mean Rhoda. I saw you listening to the cars arriving and hoping one was hers.'

Blaine gestured to the files. 'Is there anything in there you can't deal with?'

'I can deal with anything you dump on me, but I won't let you change the subject.'

He shrugged. 'We've agreed on how we feel about one another. The rest must wait until the time is appropriate.'

'Well don't wait too long. My job is on the line here.'

'Your job?' He frowned.

'Yes, my job. If Rhoda stays, Blaine Carter will continue to run this theatre with efficiency and be happy doing it. If she goes, an unhappy Blaine Carter will think of taking up one of those lucrative offers for the theatre. And there goes my job.'

He looked at her for a moment. Then he laughed out loud. He carried on laughing, unable to stop himself. 'You—you are the bloody limit.'

'Yes, so say it. Perceptive too.'

He wiped his eyes with a handkerchief, feeling the catharsis of laughter drain away his uncertainty and anxiety. He looked at her fondly. 'If she'll have me, the theatre is safe.'

'Oh, she'll have you all right. With bells on. She's had those lights in her eyes for years.' There was a knock at the door. She stood up. 'I'll lay odds that's her now.'

The door opened and Rhoda entered with her portfolio case. She stopped in the doorway.

'Sorry. Am I interrupting?'

Together they said: 'Of course not.' They looked at one another and began to laugh. Rhoda looked perplexed.

Wendy said: 'It's a little bet I had with Blaine.' She went to the door. 'I won.'

Carter stood up as she came to the desk. For a moment his mind was a blank, numbed by her mere presence. Then to cover his confusion he cleared the desk, lifted the portfolio and opened it up. Her beautifully executed drawings were exposed under the desk lamp. She bent over the desk and turned over the sheets, describing in detail her concept of the style and the placing of the furniture. Not once did she look at him. Blaine watched her and heard nothing. He saw only the fine tendrils of her hair over her ears, the soft curve of her neck and his senses responded to the delicate perfume she wore. His whole being was filled with the love he felt for her and the exquisite pain of longing, yet he knew this was not the time to speak of it. He dragged himself from his reverie and forced himself to listen.

CHAPTER EIGHTEEN

Inspector Sivo shrugged his shoulders into his coat, straightened his tie and sat at his desk, ready for his interview with Bellamy. Williams watched him, aware that Sivo never interviewed a suspect in his shirtsleeves and always, if possible, in his office. It was his way of intimidating someone he believed would try to conceal the truth.

There was a knock on the door and Constable Forrest entered.

'Mr Bellamy, sir.'

'Bring him in, Forrest.'

Forrest put his head out of the door and called: 'In here.'

Bellamy shuffled into the office, his woebegone expression evidence of his trepidation. He had been sitting in a tiny room for the best part of an hour wondering which of his many transgressions had been exposed and what misfortune awaited him at the hands of the man he feared most in the Republic of Pascua. He looked at Williams, licked his lips and watched Forrest take up a position in front of the door. He looked at the inspector, who stared at him without expression.

He tried to smile. 'Good morning, Mr Sivo.'

The inspector nodded without speaking. Then Bellamy saw the photograph in the centre of the desk. His smile froze and he quickly looked away. Beads of perspiration appeared on his forehead.

'That photograph belongs to you, I believe.' Sivo's voice was soft. 'You can take it and get out of here.'

Bellamy smiled with relief and reached for the photograph but the inspector's big hand covered it before he could snatch it up. 'Providing,' Sivo continued, 'you answer every question truthfully.'

Bellamy realized he had been stupid. His first impulse, which was to deny any knowledge of the print, was no longer an option. His face reflected his apprehension. 'What do you want to know?' He glanced at Sergeant Williams sitting at the end of the desk, pen poised over his pad ready to record every lie.

'Now,' Sivo said, looking at the ceiling speculatively. 'What do I want to know?'

The sergeant hid a smile. The boss has switched into his dramatic mode, he thought. He played up to the inspector. 'Shall I switch on the tape recorder or is this still off the record?'

'First we'll see how Mr Bellamy responds. If he becomes confused we'll record his statement and decide whether we will charge him.'

Bellamy's voice rose. 'Charge me with what? It isn't a crime to print pictures of nudes.'

Sivo's voice rasped with anger. 'No, but it is if they are used with felonious intent.'

'I never . . .'

Sivo stood up. 'I don't have time to waste. Take Mr Bellamy downstairs and charge him.'

'Wait, Mr Sivo. Ask me anything you want.'

'Do you want a lawyer present?'

'I don't need a lawyer. What do I want a lawyer for?'

Sivo took a form from his top drawer and placed it in front of Bellamy. 'Then you won't mind signing this to agree that your rights have been observed.' Bellamy took the pen eagerly and scribbled his name on the paper. 'Good. Now, I'll begin again. I warn you I know most of the answers.'

Only an idiot would fall for that, thought Williams. And this one is a monumental idiot or he wouldn't be in this mess.

'I'll tell you what you want to know, Mr Sivo. And I won't lie, I swear.'

Sivo sat back, made himself comfortable and stared at Bellamy. When the man was suitably discomforted, the inspector said: 'We will begin with the day you and your girlfriend found a mark and the two of you set him up.'

Bellamy appeared to writhe in torment, but it was merely his reluctance to admit to malfeasance that caused his distress. He had lied about his villainy for most of his life, but he knew this was the time for truth.

'She phoned to say she had a live one in her

pad. He was already stoned and she had cleaned out his wallet. She had his name and address. She asked me to come over with a camera and we could sell him the prints.'

'Blackmail him, you mean.'

Bellamy licked his lips. There was a long silence in the office but from the Bay came the mournful horn of a departing liner. They heard the whisper of the air-conditioning and the intermittent hum of the lift. Occasional bursts of laughter penetrated the closed door.

'Well?' Sivo's impatient voice was harsh. 'That's what it was, was it not?'

Bellamy nodded reluctantly. He sighed deeply. 'It was a good try, but it never came off.'

'Why not? How did you cock it up?'

'He took the picture we gave him to the tourist board offices and complained. Happens he was a bachelor and didn't care a hoot what we did with the pictures.'

Williams grinned. Sivo glared at him and turned to Bellamy. 'What happened then?'

'Nothing straight away, but a month later a fella—a real tough one—pitched up at the studio and made me an offer.'

'He did? And you couldn't refuse.' Sivo's tone was sardonic. 'What did he offer you?'

'He said if I processed the films they would send me, posted them back to a prearranged address and kept my mouth shut, I would be well paid.'

'And you never saw that man again?'

'I did. Once or twice near the small-boat basin. He never looked at me or spoke to me and I knew better than to speak to him.'

Sivo took a file from the IN tray, opened it and removed two photographs. 'Is this the man?'

Bellamy's eyes widened. 'That's him.' He looked astonished. 'How did you know?'

'Oh, we've been aware of Mr Grant for some time.' Sivo held up the second photograph. 'Have you seen this man before?'

'Everyone knows who he is. He's James Riley, top man in the tourist board. Hell, Mr Sivo, he wouldn't give me the time of day.'

'Did you ever hear from the tourist board after the man complained?'

'Never. Only from that one.' He pointed to Grant.

'I think that's all for the moment.'

'Can I go now?'

'Certainly not. Sergeant Williams will take your statement and then you will he taken to stay with friends at Pascua Petit.'

'That's where the prison is. Are you locking me up?'

'Of course. You've been a bad boy, but we'll arrange immunity if your evidence in court is satisfactory.' He gestured to Williams who took Bellamy's arm. 'It will only be a couple of weeks.'

CHAPTER NINETEEN

It took Amy several minutes to orient herself after waking from a deep drug-induced sleep. She saw the light first and then the frame that told her it was a window. Then as the details of the room swam into focus she realized she was in a hospital ward. Someone beside her was holding her hand, a fact which threw her mind into a tiny *frisson* of panic, a subconscious remnant of the terrors of the night, but then she saw the deep concern in the eyes of the one who held her hand. Her own eyes widened as recognition turned from disbelief to joy.

'Emma. How? Why? Oh Emma. Is it really you?'

'Yes, it's me.' Emma smiled. 'As to the why, well, you wrote me a letter, remember.'

Amy leaned forward and hugged her friend. 'And you came all the way across the world because you knew I needed you. No one else but you would do that.' She frowned. 'I had a dream about you. I dreamed that you were holding me; stopping me from trying to do something.'

Emma felt it wiser to move on quickly to the mundane. 'Mack is here too. He and your father spent the night here. They both left early this morning.'

'Bless them,' she said softly. 'Daddy was

here? All night?'

Emma nodded. 'He's calling at the theatre and coming back.' Her shoulder felt stiff from the long vigil. She stood up and walked to the window that overlooked a strip of lawn and the sea beyond. She turned to the girl in bed. 'No matter where you are on Pascua you can see the sea. It's wonderful. We have to travel three hundred miles from the farm to see the waves.' A thought occurred to her. 'I guess no one here advertises property "with glorious sea views". It goes without saying.'

Amy laughed. 'It's a small island. I always told you it was.'

'Yes, you did.' They both laughed. She went back to the chair beside the bed. 'Mack is coming too.' She paused, unsure of how fragile Amy's recovery was. 'Mr Sivo will be with him.'

All at once Amy's expression changed. 'Have they caught him?' she said. 'I had forgotten. Was it yesterday? The day before?' Her voice held a note of panic.

Quickly Emma took her hand. 'Hush. It's all over. There's no longer any reason to be afraid. The doctor is coming too.' She felt Amy's hand tremble.

'I'm so tired. Please stay a while.'

Emma was concerned for a moment by the rapid changes of mood, but she assumed it was the effect of the drug. 'I'll stay just as long as you want me to.'

Amy's eyes began to close and she slept.

*　　　*　　　*

It had been a long morning. Emma was still holding Amy's hand, staring vacantly at the slice of blue sky visible through the window. Her mind was blank and she would have dozed off, but for the ceaseless sounds of footsteps passing along the corridor. Some were hurried, others at a leisurely pace, while many were slow and deliberate. She had passed the long, monotonous hours putting function to footsteps. A doctor's leisurely pace on his rounds; a nurse hurrying to an emergency; a patient's slow shuffle. She had heard the distant sound of aircraft coming in to land at the airport near Rowan Point. She had gone to the window to catch an envious glance at the outgoing planes, and wondered how soon she could be on one.

She had moved to the window a few times to ease the ache in her shoulders. Twice a nurse had bustled in, looked at Amy, took her pulse and made notations on a chart. Emma was wondering whether she could ring for tea when the door opened. She recognized the doctor. Doctor—what was his name? Rapson. That was it. Slim, upright, grey-haired and handsome. His white coat was impeccable.

'Good morning, Doctor.'

'Mrs Olsen isn't it? Has Amy been awake today?'

'For a few minutes earlier this morning.'

'Good. No one else arrived yet?'

'No, Doctor. It's still a little early.'

He smiled. 'Early is on time, I always say.'

Before she could reply the door opened and Carter entered. He greeted Emma, sat beside the sleeping girl and took her hand. A few minutes later Sivo and Mack arrived with Williams in close attendance.

Doctor Rapson looked doubtfully around the crowded room. 'Do you need everybody, Inspector?'

'That's up to you, Doctor. It only needs two of us to take her statement, but she may be more comfortable with Mrs Olsen and her father present.' The doctor nodded.

Mack said: 'I'll wait in reception.' He left without waiting for a reply, relieved to be able to escape.

The voices appeared to have had an effect on Amy. She opened her eyes and gave a startled look at the inspector. She saw her father and at once her expression changed to one of delight. She hugged him and held his hand, but slowly it dawned on her that something was expected of her. Emma felt that Amy was brighter; more rested. Her eyes were clear.

Doctor Rapson sat on the end of the bed. 'The inspector would like to speak to you about the events of the night before last.'

Amy nodded. Surprisingly calm, she said: 'I

knew I would have to tell him everything eventually.'

The inspector moved his chair to the end of the bed so that he looked directly at her. 'Do you feel strong enough to do this now?' He paused. 'I must tell you that Mrs Olsen has passed on to us the two photographs you had with you on Crab Island.'

Amy was startled for a moment, then she sighed. 'Yes. I want to tell you everything.' She sounded eager. 'I know what I have to say is important and you should hear it as soon as possible.'

Carter stood up and drifted to the window. Sivo took the chair he had vacated. He said: 'This won't take long. While Sergeant Williams makes notes, I would like you to tell me everything that happened from the moment you were ready to leave the house.'

Amy looked at Emma and then at her father and as she began to speak her hand crept across the bed to take Emma's. Her voice was soft but calm.

'It began a few hours before that. It began when I found Sylvia at the stables in tears. She was reluctant to speak to me, but I persisted. Somehow I knew it concerned us all.'

The inspector said: 'Was there a cogent reason for your suspicion?'

'Nothing definite. I think I was depressed because I suspected something wasn't quite right in the tourist board, so my perceptions

247

were heightened.' She stopped and frowned. 'I really don't know what alerted me. It's something I can't express.'

'You're doing very well so far. Go on.'

'Eventually she admitted she was being blackmailed. She had gone to Crab Island a few times with a group that included Helen Summers and Ken Haig.'

Carter turned his back on the room and stared out of the window. Sivo glanced at him and back to Amy. 'Was it always with those two?'

'Yes. Haig paid her a lot of attention and it flattered her. Her mother began to object.'

'Object? How?'

'There were rows. She had words with her father too.' She looked at Carter. 'Daddy, I'm so sorry, but I have to tell them.' Emma saw the glistening tears and squeezed her hand.

Carter moved swiftly to the bed, sat on the edge and held her. 'You have to do this, my darling. It's a depressing, sorry business, but you mustn't have any compunction about speaking out.' He held her for another brief moment, then went back to the window.

'What else did Mrs Phillips tell you?'

'She said that on the last night she had gone to Crab Island, Ray Dickens poured her a drink. She took a few sips, didn't like it and put it on a table. The next thing she knew she was waking up in a bedroom.'

'I'm sorry, Amy.' Sivo's embarrassment was

palpable. 'Was she dressed? And was she . . .?'
He paused.

Amy said quickly: 'Nothing had happened.
Nothing like that, but the next day, while
shopping in the Bayside Mall, a grubby little
man thrust an envelope into her hand and
disappeared.' She paused. If she had not been
embarrassed by the inspector's question, she
was now. 'It was a nude photograph of her,
and a letter asking her if she wanted to buy the
negative. They had undressed her, posed her
for the photo, dressed her again and left her to
sleep it off.'

There was a long silence. Emma
remembered that this was the exact scenario
that Mack had described on the way back from
Crab Island when he had told her: 'I know
what this is all about.'

Emma looked at the faces around her. The
doctor was shocked. The expressions of the
two policemen were non-committal. Blaine
Carter still had his back to them.

Sivo looked at Williams, who looked up
from his pad and nodded. Sivo said: 'Go on.
What did you do then?'

'I was appalled. It was worse than I feared. I
asked her to give me the photo.'

'I will ask you to identify it later. What
happened next?'

'I stormed into Juliet's room and threw the
photograph on the bed. I demanded to know
what she knew about the vile things that were

happening on my father's island.'

'What exactly did she say?'

'At first she denied all knowledge of it, but when I said I was going to the police, she became abusive and said I was spying on her. Then she began to cry and said that at first she was not aware of what was happening on the island and when she found out it was too late. They threatened to implicate her anyway.'

'And then?'

'And then she became hysterical and attacked me. She was so violent, I just snatched up the photo and ran.' Her tears began to flow once more. Carter took her in his arms and held her. 'I'm sorry, Daddy. I had to lie to you,' she sobbed. 'I thought I was protecting you.'

After a long silence Sivo said gently: 'What did you do then?'

'I went out to the stables where Daddy found me. Then I went in to dress.'

'What time did you leave for the airport? Can you remember?'

'I went out to the garage and spoke briefly to Sylvia and then I drove out. It was exactly five minutes to nine. I always keep track of time when I'm flying out.'

Sivo looked at his notes. 'We know Mrs Phillips left at exactly nine o'clock.' He looked up. 'Mrs Olsen told us that Mrs Garland admitted that you had returned at precisely nine-sixteen. Your housekeeper looked out of

250

a window of her quarters when she heard your car.'

'With all the fuss, I had stupidly left my passport on the hall table. It wasn't there when I got back. I went straight to Mrs Garland's quarters to ask if she had moved it. She said she had put it back in my bedroom. I went back to the house.'

'Did you leave immediately?'

'Oh no. At that moment I saw a car parked alongside our boundary. I didn't think anything of it. Lovers sometimes park in the area.'

'What time was that?'

'Just on twenty past nine. I was watching the time.'

Sivo smiled encouragingly. 'You're doing fine.'

'I had just got to the door to go out to the garage when I saw a figure in the hall. I was terrified. We have never been burgled, but I knew we weren't immune. I stayed where I was, praying the man wouldn't see me.'

'That must have been just after nine-twenty. Say no later than nine twenty-five.'

Amy nodded. Emma felt her hand trembling. It was clear she was reliving the terror of that moment. Emma looked at Sivo and shook her head.

Amy interpreted the signal. 'Please don't stop,' she protested. 'There isn't much more.' She thought for a moment. 'I stood there for what seemed like an age, but it was only a few minutes. I saw the man go towards the bedrooms and about a minute later, as the study clock chimed, he came walking quickly down the passage. He was so close I saw his face.'

'Did you recognize him?'

'Of course. It was James Riley.' She rushed ahead before he could comment. 'I went to my room and the study to see if he had taken anything. Then I went to Juliet's room. She was dead.' She paused, the memory of that dark moment reflected in her eyes. 'I found her on her bed.' Amy closed her eyes.

Doctor Rapson moved to the bedside. Sivo glanced at Williams who closed his notebook.

The inspector said gently: 'Would you like to rest for a while? We can resume later.'

'No,' Amy said vehemently. 'I want to finish this.'

'Just as you wish.' Sivo nodded to Williams.

'I was terrified. I was sure he was coming back. I ran over to Mrs Garland and banged on her door. I took her back to the house. I remember rushing around putting all the lights on. At first I was going to hide on the mountain, but then I decided to go to Fran's house. The Bruneaus' house. That night I had trouble sleeping and when I did, I was engulfed in nightmares.' She made a face. 'During that night it occurred to me that Riley was using me, so I opened the envelope I had

252

to take to Sydney.' She looked at Emma. 'Well, you know what was in it. For months he had been using me as a courier for his filthy business.' She looked up at the doctor. 'I felt I couldn't trust anyone. For a while I was convinced Mr Bruneau was in the plot. I persuaded Fran to take me to Crab Island.'

Inspector Sivo closed his notebook. 'Thank you Amy. You've been very helpful and very brave.'

Amy's lips trembled. 'I'm glad that's over. Will I have to sign anything?'

'Later. Sergeant Williams will come and see you tomorrow with a statement.' He stood up. 'We'll leave you now. Have a good rest.' There was a long pause as he looked around the room. 'Each one of you is here because you were required to assist Amy in your personal capacity. Nothing you heard here today may be repeated. Thank you for being here.'

Emma listened to him with surprise. His demeanour was strangely, almost embarrassingly, formal, at odds with the kind, considerate and patient way he had handled Amy's interview. Perhaps, she thought, he had been affected, as she had been, by the testimony they had just heard.

Sivo went out to his car and sat for several minutes looking over Southern Beach. Williams watched his face. The inspector was an angry man. Finally Sivo said: 'Think of what that child went through. She discovered that her family is enmeshed in a blackmail ring; she sees a photograph of her friend as a victim, is beaten by her stepmother, finds her murdered and then sees her employer sneaking out of the house. No wonder she went over the edge.' He shook his head. 'I can't wait to pick up those bastards.' He turned on the ignition. 'Not yet. Soon. We have a final chore to complete.'

In his office, Sivo did not take time to remove his coat but went straight to his desk. Williams closed the door behind him. Sivo picked up the telephone.

'While I make this call, I want you to locate Glasspoole.'

'At Uva Point?'

'No. Not Captain Barry Glasspoole. I want his brother, Richard Glasspoole.' Sivo looked at his watch. 'You may find him at the Hunt Club at this time of the morning. If not, ask someone where you can find him.' He dialled as Williams pulled the other phone towards him.

With the ringing tone sounding in his ear, the inspector sat back wearily and swivelled his chair to gaze out at the vista he loved. To look at the ever-changing sea was almost as pleasant as being out there with snorkel and flippers, hunting the edible species of the deep. Far more productive, he thought, than hunting human predators.

'Carter residence.' Mrs Garland's voice

jerked him from his reverie.

'Sivo, here, Mrs Garland. Do you know if Mr Martin is at home?'

'Yes he is, Mr Sivo. But he's out exercising the horses in the paddock. You won't get him on the telephone now.'

'Thank you, Mrs Garland.' He caught her attention before she could replace the receiver. 'Just one more question, Mrs Garland.'

'Yes sir.' The rising inflection was evidence of her curiosity.

'On the day of the—um—the day Mrs Carter died, did you clean her room? You know, dust and polish the ornaments?'

'Of course I did. I do any occupied bedrooms daily and the others once a week.'

'What time did you do Mrs Carter's room that day?'

Pause. 'At about two o'clock. She got up late, had some—ah—refreshment, and then went back to bed.'

'So she had no visitors before Amy went in to her?'

'No. I would have known.'

'Thank you Mrs Garland. You've been very helpful. Would you mind making a supplementary statement for me later?'

'About the cleaning?'

'Yes. Williams will come and see you.'

'Certainly, Inspector.'

Sivo put down the telephone and sighed. 'All

too easy,' he murmured.

'Sir?'

'It won't be long now, Sergeant.'

'If you say so, sir.' Williams handed him the other telephone. 'Mr Glasspoole, sir.'

'Sivo here, Dick. I won't keep you. I know how busy you are. Just two quick questions.'

The questions were asked and answered, and the inspector replaced the handset gently on its cradle.

CHAPTER TWENTY

It was a sombre group that assembled in the Prime Minister's Mansion at the end of Pearl Drive. Sivo and his superior officer, Police Commissioner Gordon Harper, had arrived to find John Bowden, the Attorney-General, staring moodily at the bathers far below on Pearl Beach.

He turned to greet them.

'Nasty business.'

The commissioner nodded. He eased his overweight body into the easy chair at the left of the desk.

Bowden cleared his throat. He was short, white-haired and distinguished-looking. He said. 'Damage control is essential.' Sivo remained silent. He walked to the window and looked out and up. Clouds were drifting, but in the wrong direction for rain.

The door opened and the Prime Minister entered. Paul Geddes greeted them with a cheerfulness that was lacking in the others. He was a big man with thick, grey hair. Blunt and forthright, he ran an honest administration. The electorate loved him, returning his party with monotonous regularity. It was common knowledge that his party hung on his coat tails, but the voters cared nothing for parties as long as 'Saint Paul' was in office. The opposition, the Independence Freedom Party, had won independence for Pascua a hundred years ago, but they had grown listless while waiting for Paul Geddes to retire.

He was a down-to-earth man who refused to live in the Mansion. He used it for conferences, special occasions and dinners which were hosted by his wife Elaine. At night he went back to his modest home overlooking the cove at Lea Buka. He had three loves; Elaine, snorkelling and deep-sea fishing. His deep tan testified to his hours in and on the sea. They had three sons who had positioned themselves in important jobs in different parts of the world.

He was the despair of the security section, refusing protection or bodyguards. He was often heard to remark: 'The island is lousy with my relatives and friends. Who the hell is going to kill me?'

He sat in the impressive chair behind his

desk.

'For God's sake, Joe, sit down. I can't keep looking up at you.'

Sivo smiled and relaxed in the chair at the end of the desk. Geddes looked at each of them in turn.

'Well, I hope one of you has a solution to this mess. Those bastards could kill our tourist trade.'

The commissioner looked at the inspector and nodded. Sivo took a deep breath. He had a solution, but he wasn't sure if it would be acceptable to the others. He began to summarize Amy Carter's evidence.

Geddes stopped him. 'Is there nothing on paper?'

The Attorney-General shook his head. 'Not advisable at this stage. Best to work out a strategy first and I'll see whether it's legal.' Geddes nodded and looked at Sivo who began to talk. He outlined the scope of the blackmail plot, continued with his summary of Amy's story and set out a timeline for the arrests of the culprits.

When he had finished Geddes sat for a moment deep in thought. Then he said: 'That girl has guts. Never liked that woman Blaine married. Now perhaps Elaine will start asking Blaine to the Prime Minister's Mansion again.'

The three men were not surprised at the Prime Minister's comments. They knew he always cleared the trivial from his thoughts, leaving himself space for his incisive mind to work out solutions.

Sivo said: 'May I make a suggestion?'

'I'm sorry Joe. I know what's best for Pascua. I see the holistic view, and while I know you have our best interests at heart, I want to preserve our biggest money-spinner.' He looked out of the window. 'Thank God for our forebears. They devised a constitution that's the envy of the Pacific.' He looked back at them. 'Let us use it.'

Sivo smiled inwardly. He knew what was coming. Geddes was going to outline Sivo's own solution.

'We have an asset-forfeiture clause; we have the right in this office to decide on an appropriate penalty with the approval of the judiciary; and no one not born here can ever become a Pascuan National. Non-residents may live here on a permit as long as they wish, providing they behave themselves.' He looked at Bowden. 'I think that covers it, John.'

Bowden nodded. 'What you're suggesting, if I read you correctly, is that we offer him a deal.'

Exactly, thought Sivo.

Geddes nodded. 'Either he pleads guilty and gets off with a light six months and we take everything he owns, or he pleads not guilty, he has his trial, we ask for the maximum and he goes for twenty years and we still get his assets.' He looked at Sivo. 'That was your solution, wasn't it Joe?'

Sivo smiled. 'Yes sir.' No wonder this man had lasted for twenty years in the job. The commissioner had spent no more than twenty minutes on the phone briefing him. 'I want to put him off a boat in Sydney with only a suit and shoes.'

'Are any of the others nationals?'

'Only one. A man named Bellamy.' Sivo frowned. 'But we need him as a key witness anyway. We'll have to offer him something.'

'The other four?'

Bowden said: 'The same deals, but no jail time. Just heavy fines. We don't want to try anyone who pleads not guilty. We don't want a media circus. We want them off the island as quickly as possible.'

'You've identified all the victims?'

Sivo looked grim. 'Not yet, but we will.'

'This is what I suggest.' Geddes swivelled his chair once and back. He was enjoying himself. 'We compensate them for their losses, offer them a free fortnight in Pascua or any other destination of their choice.' He paused. 'In return for their discretion, of course. Make up some sort of contract, John.'

Bowden smiled. 'I will, but I'm sure it won't be necessary. They're not likely to take those photos to the papers.' He clipped his pen to his pocket and folded the paper on which he had been making notes. 'That island of Carter's. Do you think . . .'

The Prime Minister cut him short. 'Don't even think about it. Do we consider depriving a family of its home because it's been burgled?' He shook his head. 'No, this is exactly what has happened here. Some scummy characters have betrayed his trust. Besides, there's that constitution I talked about.'

Bowden shrugged. 'It was just a thought.'

'I won't countenance it.' He stared at the window. 'I remember taking that girl—Amy Carter—snorkelling once. She was about thirteen. We came out of the water and sat in the sun and she began to speak about Crab Island. She loves that place and is crazy about the crabs, the octopus colonies and the birds. Wanted to turn it into a nature reserve. Even asked Blaine to tear the house down so that the wild life wouldn't be disturbed. She went on about the coconut crab becoming extinct all over the Pacific.' He smiled. 'Although that may have been dislike of the types Juliet Carter was entertaining there.'

He stopped and looked at the three men. 'Sorry. Here I am running on when you lot have work to do.' He looked at Sivo. 'We haven't talked about the murder. Are you ready to charge anyone?'

'I'm not sure I have enough . . .'

Bowden interrupted him. 'I couldn't indict on the evidence Joe has at present. We can place people at the scene but the evidence is too flimsy to make a case to take to Vicente's court.'

Sivo shrugged. 'I'm sorry, sir, but placing someone at the scene isn't enough to call him or her a killer. The investigation is proceeding.'

Geddes nodded. 'I understand, but don't let it drag on. It seems to me that we should finalize the two cases together. Please make it fast. My secretary has signed requisitions for twenty-two extra men to work on the case. Section heads are bitching to her about being short-handed.' He stood up. 'That's it then.' He looked at Bowden. 'See that everything is tied up tightly. We don't want Judge Vicente setting him free on a technicality.' He looked thoughtfully at the window. 'To think we nearly had that piece of shit here for the Commemoration Dinner.' He looked at Sivo. 'We're going to be two guests short come Saturday.' His tone was bantering. 'What about you, Joe? Join us for dinner?'

The inspector shifted uncomfortably. 'We— I—I never know where I'll be.' He tried levity. 'There may be a terrorist threat to one of the cruise liners.'

Geddes laughed out loud. 'You lying sod. You just don't want to put on the soup and fish.' He walked them to the door. 'You'll come round eventually. I'll get Ethel to help me.'

The fingerprint results arrived on his desk just as the inspector took off his coat. He looked at them and put them aside to read forensic's analysis of the soil samples.

'Hmm. It seems our soil sample from Carter's house is not as exclusive as we thought. Pity. The same soil exists at Largo and Bougainville.' He looked thoughtful. 'Unless he didn't . . .' Sivo paused.

'Sir?'

He put the paper aside. 'We can still make it work for us.' He stood up and stretched. He gazed out to sea where the setting sun tinted the swells running in to shore. 'I'll get out for a few days fishing by weekend.' He turned. 'Where is Riley now?'

'In the interrogation room. He's been there half an hour. Steamed up he is.'

'Good. That's how I like them. Bring him up.'

'Up here, sir?'

'Up here. I'm looking forward to this.'

Blaine Carter parked in his slot in the car-park, switched off the engine and looked up at the bronze-brick Victorian pile. For a long time now he had not thought of what the theatre represented financially. Now he did.

Perversely because he was aware of what he would be turning down when he rejected the latest offer from an Australian consortium. Of course much depended on the outcome of a discussion he intended having with Rhoda Larkin. As he thought of her, he was filled with a new zeal. His world was being turned around by the knowledge that Amy was safe, Rhoda would be staying on and he would be rid of the parasites that had fed on his success. How could he have been so blind?

The inspector was due to arrive after the play ended to arrest four of his company. He was certain that three of them would be his accountants and Haig, but he could only guess at the fourth. Helen Summers? Clearly it was someone who had been at the Crab Island parties. He shrugged. Whoever it was, he would be well rid of them.

He hurried through the theatre and up the stairs to his office. Rhoda had preceded him and smiled as he entered.

He stopped, overwhelmed once again by the happiness he felt and the sheer joy of her presence. He had an impulse to take her in his arms, but resisted the urge. He was astonished therefore when she walked up to him and hugged him. He beamed. 'Now that's what I call appropriate.'

'Oh damn it, Blaine. What we're doing is silly. Acting out some hypocritical convention which neither of us cares about.'

'I could not have put it better.'

She went back to her portfolio. 'Enough of this wild abandon. Let's get down to work.'

*   *   *

Riley walked into Sivo's office, his collar rumpled, a shdow on his chin and a hunted look on his face. A charge of cruising without running lights was a serious matter in Pascua. He was unaware of just how serious the actual charges were. He began to bluster the moment he saw the inspector at his desk.

'Dammit Sivo, I know my man was stupid, but is it necessary for me to submit to this humiliating treatment? I've been waiting . . .'

'Sit down.' Sivo's voice was sharply authoritative. 'Just keep your mouth shut and wait until I speak to you.' He took a paper from his desk drawer. 'I am going to put some serious charges to you. Do you want your lawyer present?'

'What the hell do I want with a lawyer?'

'If that means you don't want a lawyer then sign this. Just so that I can't be accused of violating your rights.' Flustered, Riley grabbed the waiver and signed it.

'See here Sivo. I won't . . .'

'Do as you're told.'

Williams sat with his pad open, his pen at the ready. In all the time he had worked with the inspector, he had never seen him react to a

265

suspect as he did now. Sivo had often told him of the dangers of becoming personally involved in an investigation, but he had obviously succumbed to the combination of Amy's plight and his distaste for blackmailers.

Sivo looked at Riley for a long time. Then he said: 'When did you last go to Largo or Bougainville?'

'Not for years. My boat . . .'

'You will swear to that?'

'Of course. My boat . . .'

'I'm not interested in your boat.'

'You're not?' Riley was surprised, aware suddenly that this was more serious than his skipper's dereliction.

'Where were you between the hours of nine and ten on the night before last? The tenth of this month. The night Juliet Carter was murdered.'

Riley's eyes widened with shock. All at once he knew he was in trouble. He knew where he was at that time.

'Look. If this is about Juliet's murder . . .'

'Just answer the question.' The inspector waited a moment for him to answer. 'I have to warn you that several factors place you in Mrs Carter's bedroom at the time she was murdered.'

Riley realized it was useless to lie. 'All right. I was there, but she was dead when I arrived there.'

'Why did you change the tyres on your car

as soon as you knew we had a tyre-track?'

'I—I was afraid—I didn't want to . . .'

'The tyres don't really matter. We have a witness who saw you leaving Juliet Carter's bedroom at the critical time.'

'A witness. Who?' He shrugged. 'Oh hell, it doesn't matter. I was there, but I swear I did not kill her.'

'Right. Let's change the subject. I want to discuss nude photos taken at Crab Island.'

Riley swore. 'I had nothing to do with those.'

Sivo sighed with exasperation, rose from his desk and walked around the office. Williams knew this was his superior's strategy to drag out the tension. Sivo went back to his desk. 'Let me ask you again. Did you not arrange for Bellamy to process your photographs?'

Finally Riley realized he was done for, but he had to make one last effort to retrieve the situation.

'I merely offered certain people the opportunity to purchase souvenirs of their stay.'

'The senator said you asked for a hundred thousand United States dollars a throw.'

Riley was silent.

'Don't be stupid, Riley.'

Riley shrugged. 'It was worth a try.' He looked at Sivo, pleadingly. 'What are you going to do?'

'It's not my call.' Sivo stood up and walked

to the window. He stared out at the dying sun as it threw a fiery glow on the eastern sky. He looked up at the sky. Still no sign of rain.

He spoke without turning. 'You're not leaving here a free man, Riley.' He turned. 'James Riley, I am placing you under arrest on a charge of blackmail.'

'Oh God. Is there nothing I can say?' Riley's face was beaded with perspiration.

The inspector sat at his desk. 'The Prime Minister is particularly distressed about what this will do to the tourist industry. He asked the Attorney-General to offer you a deal.'

Riley brightened. 'I'll do anything.'

'Plead guilty, prevent a trial and you'll do six months and your assets will be forfeited. It's generous considering the penalty for blackmail is twenty years; and you lose your assets anyway.'

'What if I decide to take my chances with the Judge?'

'Let me tell you what we've got and it will help you decide.' He ticked off the facts on his fingers. 'Grant will make a statement naming you as the organizer. Bellamy . . .'

'I never dealt with Bellamy.'

Sivo continued as though Riley hadn't spoken. 'Bellamy dealt with Grant. There is the link. We are arresting the four at the Carter Theatre after the show tonight.' He smiled sardonically. 'Do you imagine for one moment they will cover for you?'

Riley's eyes closed. 'I haven't a choice.'

'No.' There was a long silence. 'What possessed you to hide the prints in the attic at Crab Island?'

'There was nowhere else. They were well hidden, and besides it implicated Juliet Carter and kept her in line.'

'She wasn't involved at first, was she?'

'No. And it was a mistake to involve her at all. When Amy Carter confronted her she rang me to say that she was going to spill everything to her husband.'

'So that's why you went out there.'

'Only to talk sense into her. I didn't kill her.'

Sivo was non-committal. 'The Attorney-General is waiting for your answer.'

'What choice do I have?'

The inspector smiled wolfishly. 'Absolutely none.'

*   *   *

The other conspirators were arrested when the curtain came down for the last time on *The Long Summer*. Blaine watched the curtain calls with a sense of relief. It had not been a happy play for him. It reflected too much of what he himself had suffered. Sitting in the VIP box with Rhoda Larkin, he felt that this was the beginning of a new season for him; a season in which he would convince Amy that he was, after all, someone she could depend on. He looked at Rhoda, took her hand and smiled.

The four were taken away in two police vehicles, Haig and Helen Summers loudly proclaiming their intention to sue the Republic of Pascua. Perry and Dickens were sullen and defiant. Rhoda watched them go with distaste.

'It makes me feel we have to call in the fumigators.'

CHAPTER TWENTY-ONE

Emma walked through the stable yard savouring the familiar smells of oats, horses and polished leather. If she closed her eyes she could have been amongst her own stables on Cold Water Farm. She was overwhelmed by a moment of homesickness before she recalled that she and Mack would he boarding the early morning flight on the first leg of their journey home. In two days she would be in her own stables amongst her own horses and Teig and Grampa would be there to greet them. Now that Amy was recovering and Blaine's problems were solved, there was really no need for them to stay. She cared nothing for the mystery of Juliet Carter's murder. The chief suspect was in custody, but Mack had told her he was sceptical about the prospects of convicting him. He felt there were too many unanswered questions. Well, she thought, perhaps those were the answers Inspector Sivo would be seeking when he called on them this morning.

She looked up at the mountain. It was a compelling feature of the landscape and she was constrained to look up each time she was outdoors. Emma did not think she liked that. It was unnatural somehow, as though it was standing up there saying: 'Look at me. You have to look at me.'

Emma smiled at the thought. She must be suffering from mountain fever. She wondered if Amy ever felt the pull of the mountain. It was lovely enough, with the same ambience of her home valley, but to live here would eventually turn her claustrophobic, hemmed in, as it were, by the sea. Nowhere to go in any direction.

Her musing was cut short by the arrival of two cars and the slow opening of the electrically operated gates. She gave one last pat to a soft nose nuzzling her and went back into the house.

Mrs Garland met her in the hall. 'Please go to the study, Mrs Olsen. They're all waiting.'

All? How many were there, she wondered? Her question was answered by a crowded study. The inspector and the sergeant were being regarded by a group which included Mack, Mr and Mrs Martin, Blaine Carter and, to fill any empty spaces, Mrs Garland and herself. A blackboard on an easel stood against the fireplace. She recognized the blackboard as one that she had seen in the spare room. Probably a pre-teen present.

There was a general shuffling as everyone found somewhere to sit. The sergeant sat at the end of the desk and opened his pad. The inspector stood in front of the assembled group.

He wasted no time on pleasantries. 'My purpose for being here today is to ask for answers to supplementary questions that have arisen.' Emma saw Mack's eyebrows lift in his customary expression of disbelief. Sivo continued, 'I have here a timetable and I hope some of you may clarify one or two points. Unfortunately Amy is not here, but we can accept the facts she has given us. That goes for Mrs Phillips too.'

'I should hope so.' Gerda Martin's acerbic tone emphasized her dislike of the inspector.

He ignored her. 'I have a timetable for the movements of all the people who were here on the night Juliet Carter was murdered. I hope you will comment on anything with which you disagree.'

A precise man, Emma thought appreciatively. A bit like Grampa, only my grampa is unique, she told herself proudly. Once more she felt a pang of homesickness. She was aware that the inspector was addressing the blackboard. He wrote:

8.55 p.m. Amy Carter leaves for the airport.

9.00 p.m. Mrs Phillips leaves for the airport.

He turned to the assembly. 'No quarrel with that?' There was no reply.

9.10 p.m. Juliet Carter is murdered.
(This time is accurate within a minute or two.)

There was a surprised murmur, then a shocked silence. Blaine Carter frowned. 'How can you be so precise?'
'Bear with me. The time is self-explanatory.' He wrote:

9.16 p.m. Amy returns for passport. Not on hall table. Goes to Mrs Garland.

Mack looked puzzled. 'Did Amy go over to Mrs Garland's apartment?'
'Yes, she did.' Sivo continued with his timetable.

9.23 p.m. James Riley arrives.

9.25 p.m. Amy re-enters the house.

9.27 p.m. Amy sees Riley leaving Juliet's room.

9.32 p.m. Amy finds Juliet dead.

9.35 p.m. Amy calls Mrs Garland.

11.00 p.m. Amy leaves for the Bruneaus' home.

The inspector put the chalk on the mantelpiece and brushed his fingers. 'Anyone see anything wrong with that?' There was a general murmur. 'One at a time, please. Blaine?'

'You believe Riley arrived after Juliet was dead.'

'Yes indeed.'

'But he was your prime suspect.'

'He was never my suspect. Riley and his four sleazy friends were blackmailers, but I never suspected any of them of murder.'

Gerda's thin mouth tightened. 'I suppose you are suggesting my daughter had something to do with it?'

The inspector's eyes widened. 'Why on earth would I believe that? Oh no. The killer came in to get the negatives of some photographs, and when Juliet would not co-operate, she was attacked. She was probably strangled unintentionally. Then Amy returned and the killer hid. The killer was about to search the room when Riley arrived. He says he heard a rustle of silk. The killer remained in hiding until the house was quiet. It was then

274

that the room was trashed. Neither Riley nor Amy saw any disturbance in the room when they saw the body.' He looked at Gerda. 'No, Mrs Martin. Why should I implicate your daughter when I have the killer right here.'

There was a shocked silence. He's toying with us, Emma thought, and he's enjoying it. She regarded him with disapproval.

Gerda Martin said: 'Then why did you prevent her from taking her plane?'

'Because I was not sure who the murderer was then. But you, Mrs Martin, told me that you were the killer.'

'I certainly did not.' Her voice had risen to a shriek.

'In your daughter's hotel room you said: "Sylvia could not have murdered Juliet, smashed the mirror, broken the vase and trashed the room in a mere five minutes". How did you know the mirror and the vase were broken and the room trashed, Mrs Martin?'

'Why—I—I saw it.'

'When? That room has been sealed since the murder. It's still sealed. When did you see it?'

'Somebody told me. I—I can't remember who.'

'The only people who knew are here and they were sworn to silence.' He made an ostentatious gaze around the room. 'Which of you told Mrs Martin that?'

There was a frozen silence. No one looked at Gerda Martin.

Harry Martin said: 'That's not evidence. You can't accuse Gerda . . .'

'By itself it's not evidence. But her fingerprints are on the base of the vase she broke.'

'I've often handled that vase.'

'I doubt it, but your claim is irrelevant. You see, Mrs Garland cleaned that vase a couple of hours before the murder. She gave it a good rub and the only fingerprints on it were yours and hers.'

Harry Martin refused to accept it. 'How do you know it wasn't her—Mrs Garland?'

Sivo smiled grimly. 'The killer was at Crab Island early the next morning looking for photographs of Sylvia Phillips, two of which you dropped when you fell, Mrs Martin.'

'I was at the Hunt Club.'

'That was where you said you would be, but Mr Glasspoole, the Hunt Club manager, recorded your arrival at eleven-thirty.' He turned then to Sergeant Williams; clearly by pre-arrangement, Williams handed Sivo the nude picture of Sylvia Phillips. He held it up. 'Is this what you were looking for, Mrs Martin?'

Afterwards, Emma realized that this was the catalyst that enraged the woman out of her obstinate calm. The inspector had staged the whole thing. Emma had to admire his strategy though she deplored it. The woman gave a shriek of anger and lunged for Sivo. 'That bitch ruined my daughter's marriage. I'll kill you as I killed her.' She was still screaming when she was led away.

It was then that Williams remembered the inspector's reference to the motive and a biblical king. Solomon knew the power of a mother's love.

> Hungry Mountain
> Republic of Pascua

Dearest, Dearest Emma,

How can I express all the gratitude I feel for your instant and unselfish response to my somewhat incoherent letter to you. Left to myself I don't know if I would have survived on Crab Island. Yours was the reaction of true friendship.

Today Riley, Perry and Dickens were carted off to Pascua Petit, and Haig and Summers were put on a plane to other climes. We are well rid of them.

Daddy is seeing an awful lot of a certain lady, and appears to be gloriously happy. She is one of a kind, thoughtful and honest and I adore her. They have no plans yet, but there is no need to rush into anything.

Speaking of plans, our cute Sergeant Williams and my school-friend Sally MacIntosh have set a date. Why does that word 'date' remind me of something? Oh yes. Sheldon Sivo has asked me out. It's true. He's dishy, but any intentions I may have had must be put on hold. Uncle Paul (who else has a Prime Minister as an honorary uncle?) has asked me if I would like funding for my idea of turning Crab into a nature reserve. He said we can accommodate fourteen visitors in the house and still have room for Daddy and me. Daddy loves the idea. I'll have to think about it. I'm not sure about letting people loose on the island and disturbing all my beautiful crabs.

Poor Mrs Martin is being held at the hospital. Daddy does not think she will ever be fit to stand trial. I used to wonder about her; always uncomfortable in her presence. Harry Martin accepted a position at the Hunt Club after Daddy sold off the horses. It was for the best. We don't ride any more.

Mrs Garland asks about you often, wondering when you are coming back to visit. I suggested that as you never paid your bed-and-board bill when you left, we should send you a summons. She said if that was the only way to get you here, then so be it. Go for it. Who would have thought my darling Nanny Garland had a sense of humour. She laughs a lot now, and sometimes I actually hear her singing.

She keeps asking when Rhoda is coming to stay.

Daddy adds his love and gratitude to mine.

Ever your devoted

Amy.